THE THIRD HOLE

The DeLuca Series

THE THIRD HOLE

The DeLuca Series

*Dear Rosemary,
It is so good to see you.
Patti Starr*

PATTI STARR

IGUANA

Copyright © 2013 Patti Starr
Published by Iguana Books
720 Bathurst Street, Suite 303
Toronto, Ontario, Canada
M5V 2R4

All rights reserved. No part of this publication may be reproduced, stored in a retrieval system or transmitted, in any form or by any means, electronic, mechanical, recording or otherwise (except brief passages for purposes of review) without the prior permission of the author or a licence from The Canadian Copyright Licensing Agency (Access Copyright). For an Access Copyright licence, visit www.accesscopyright.ca or call toll free to 1-800-893-5777.

Publisher: Greg Ioannou
Front cover image: Jane Goodwin, Stuart Starr
Front cover design: Jane Goodwin, Stuart Starr
Book layout design: Meghan Behse

Library and Archives Canada Cataloguing in Publication

Starr, Patti
    The third hole / Patti Starr.

(The DeLuca series)
Issued also in electronic formats.
ISBN 978-1-927403-59-4

  I. Title. II. Series: Starr, Patti. DeLuca series.

PS8587.T3288T45 2013   C813'.54   C2013-901498-5

This is an original print edition of *The Third Hole*.

Other books in
The DeLuca Series

Deadly Justice

Final Justice

ACKNOWLEDGEMENTS

My thanks to Iguana Books: Greg Ioannou – the boss – who was there seventeen years ago when my first novel, *Deadly Justice,* was published, and to his wonderful team, Emily Niedoba, my cover designer Jane Goodwin, my copy editor Alexa Caruso, and particularly Meghan Behse, who worked on the edit with me. Her patience and expertise were so important.

Beresheet – Jack Stoddart, Don Bastian and Rosemary Aubert – you were the beginning. Thank you.

Kudos to two dynamite chicks and one fabulous hunk:

Detective Nadine Teeft, whose investigative expertise and creative insight into the minds of creepy criminals ensured that the plot was always credible;

Debra Snider, one of Ontario's top criminal lawyers, who provided the legal perspective and murderous alternatives; and

Stuart Starr, whose social media/internet skills and strong shoulders helped to make it happen – Stu, you are simply the best!

This book is dedicated to my wonderful family – a family that now includes grandchildren who will love seeing their names in print:

Max, Zoe, Koby, Jacob, Rachel, Jona, Leora, James and Gabrielle.

You have made my life so much better. I love you.

PROLOGUE

Boston, Massachusetts. December 31, 1999.

"Would you like another drink, sir?" asked the steward as he rolled the liquor cart up to Grant Teasdale's seat on the aisle. "This is the last call before we land in Boston."

"Yes, thanks. I'll have another scotch and soda."

Grant looked at his watch. *I should be at Elizabeth's house before eight o'clock.*

He had been a little uneasy about going back to Boston, particularly to the home of the late Santino DeLuca, once head of the Villano crime family. The memories of his last visit there, and of Rebecca, wouldn't be easy for him to handle. But Elizabeth DeLuca's phone call had been so upbeat that he had accepted her invitation to come and celebrate the new millennium with her family.

Grant thought back to his sudden departure almost two years earlier. He cringed, as he always did, when he remembered the madness. It had been six weeks after Rebecca's death and her daughter Lisa had called him, crying and frightened. He had been drinking, again, but he rushed over to her house, or at least tried to rush over. He hadn't been fit to drive and had to walk the ten blocks in a freezing snowstorm.

"Lisa, where are you?" I called as I pushed open the front door and took off my boots and heavy jacket. There was silence. I called

again. When I heard her crying I raced up the stairs, except in my condition I kept stumbling, and at the top I tripped over a chair.

"Oh Grant, I'm an orphan!" she cried when I reached her room. "When I was seven years old my grandfather died and Mom cried the same words to me. I'm afraid – I don't know what to do."

"I know how you feel," I answered, trying to shake off the throbbing in my head as I sat down next to her. "I've been an orphan since I was ten years old. Here, put your head on my shoulder and we'll tell each other jokes."

When Grant had awoke a few hours later wrapped in a sheet with Lisa, he had little recollection of how, and what had happened, only that they were both naked. He couldn't remember why he had kissed her or why she had kissed him back. Were they just two mourners clinging to each other, needing a reminder that they were still alive? Or had he been so drunk that he didn't think about what he was doing?

For the first time in his life, Grant Teasdale, former cop, former FBI/RCMP Inspector, had run away, unable to cope with the emotional chaos that had become his life. He had gone back to Pt. St. Lucie, Florida, to his houseboat and his business. He worked twelve hours a day, and whenever his memories became too painful he turned to the bottle. He tried to wipe out what had happened between him and Lisa as just a drunken dream, but he knew that he was in denial and was ashamed that he never had the guts to call or face her again.

He always told himself: *No rationale can make what I have just done acceptable, but Elizabeth is going to look after her. She is in good hands. I would only be a reminder of a terrible mistake.*

The plane made a sharp turn. He gulped down the rest of his drink and leaned back in the seat. His business was booming, his son Kevin was living well in a group home, his parents were getting older, but could still manage independently, and his brother Larry, whom he worried about, was still living alone in Toronto.

Larry has never gotten over Elizabeth, thought Grant as the plane started its descent, *just as I will never get over Rebecca.*

On his way out of the terminal, he stopped at a flower shop to pick up some roses for Elizabeth and then walked over to buy a bottle of champagne. He handed the attendant a one hundred dollar bill and while he waited for the change, he glanced through the local newspaper. There was a screaming headline about the drug trade and two bullet ridden bodies found near the Charles River.

So what, he thought. *New faces, new deals. The game never changes, only the people who play. And my Rebecca? She'll still be gone and I will still be alone.*

Ten minutes later he was in a cab heading towards Brimmer Street in the Beacon Hill section of Boston. He stretched his legs and watched the familiar lights of the city get closer.

At eight o'clock Grant was standing outside the DeLuca town house overwhelmed with memories.

Suddenly the door opened and a smiling Elizabeth threw her arms around him. "Grant, how nice it is to see you again! I'm so glad you're here."

She took his arm and led him into the den where he was warmly welcomed by the DeLuca brothers – Matthew, now a seminary student who was as jovial as ever and Peter, rumoured to be following in his late father's footsteps. Peter was somehow different from the last time Grant had seen him.

"Inspector, this is Angela Brattini," said Peter as his arm tightened around a young woman with black hair and even blacker saucer eyes. *Still drop-dead gorgeous,* thought Grant as she smiled at him.

"Angela, how nice to see you again," said Grant as he took her hand. "We met briefly at Santino's memorial mass."

"That was three years ago," said Angela, "a lifetime."

"Yes, a lifetime," said a familiar voice from the doorway.

Grant spun around. It was Lisa, holding a little boy with red hair and blue eyes. He stood frozen on the spot and couldn't take his eyes off the boy. When he finally looked at Lisa her warm smile told him all that he needed to know.

"Would you like to hold him?" she asked. "His name is Sam."

Grant held out his arms, unable to speak.

"Come everyone, let's go in for dinner," said Elizabeth. "A new year is coming and we have so much to celebrate!"

CHAPTER ONE

Pt. St. Lucie, Florida.

"Aw come on Dad, don't be such a nerd!"

"Nice way to talk to your old man," said Grant, trying hard not to smile. "You know that I'm not interested in Facebook or Twitter or tweeting or blogging or whatever else the rage of the moment is."

"But this is the way of life today," laughed Sam, his eyes dancing. "You can check out what's hot – and maybe even get a line on some chick. I know you are getting close to the big six-o, but who knows? Maybe certain body parts will still work for you with the right partner. Time is running out!"

"What?" howled Grant as he reached out to wrap his arm around Sam's neck. "Them's fighting words. How come a little kid like you has sex on the brain? I don't remember giving you any birds and bees lessons."

"I don't live in prehistoric times like you did, father dear," yelped Sam as he tried to get out of his father's grip. "We all know everything about everything, and what we don't know, we can find out soon enough."

Grant couldn't stop smiling. Sam was already up to his shoulder and his red hair and blue eyes made him almost his clone. Grant Teasdale was six feet tall with wide shoulders and a very thick neck. He looked as if he could have been a linebacker for the Dolphins. His once flaming-red hair was speckled with white, but his blue eyes were still incredible.

"Okay, enough of this conversation," he said still poking Sam. "You have plenty of work to do, which you have been avoiding. I promised your mother that if she let you stay with me for an extra week I would make sure that you practiced your bar mitzvah stuff.

"Do you want me to get in trouble with her?" Grant went on, laughing. "Do you want her to be mad at me? June 30th is only three months away. So I now decree that you are going to spend tomorrow in your room practising so that when you go home next week, you will be close to perfect."

"I will be perfect," answered Sam his blue eyes flashing and a big smile on his face. "I have the best of both worlds – a Catholic father and a Jewish mother. So I can't be anything other than perfect. At least that's what Nonna Elizabeth tells me."

"Well, if anyone should know the real facts, it's Nonna Elizabeth, for sure," said a smiling Grant. "Okay, now we have to get going. I don't want Kevin to start getting agitated if we're late."

Kevin was living in the Christopher Robin Group Home, one of the best in the country for the developmentally handicapped. It was located in Hallandale, a few miles north of Miami Beach, but it was over a two-hour drive from Grant's houseboat in Pt. St. Lucie.

Brain damaged at birth, Kevin would never mature emotionally beyond the level of a ten-year-old even with the best professional input. According to the doctors, the umbilical cord had been twisted around his neck during the delivery, cutting off his oxygen supply. "God's will," the priest had said at the time. But Grant wasn't so sure. He feared that somehow he had passed along a curse to his son.

When Grant had taken early retirement from the RCMP, he had moved to Pt. St. Lucie, Florida with his late wife Doris and his son Kevin. He established his own security firm known for its efficient and discreet service – as well as its excellent contacts with international law enforcement agencies, particularly the FBI. His skills and his reputation had made him very popular with certain secretive Latin Americans who wanted to travel back and forth between Florida and Argentina without any hassles, accompanied by their money. His company was also known for its access to the Russians – though their power was not as it had once been. The Chinese had quickly become the flavour of the month, but Grant wasn't ready to put the time and effort into changing his priorities and seeking their business. He was doing very well with his regulars, thank you very much.

But Grant knew that he had to make some changes in his life sooner or later. Even though he really loved his houseboat – the gentle sounds of the water lapping against the boat's hull, the squawking of the seagulls early in the morning, the cool breezes even during the hot spells – he knew that it was time to make the move to Palm Beach. His clients would have easier access to him, Kevin would only be forty-five minutes away and Sam, the light of his life, could make some appropriate friends during his frequent visits from his home in Boston.

"Dad, do you think there is any chance that Kevin will ever get better?" asked Sam as they drove along the Florida Turnpike in Grant's red Buick convertible. They both loved the wind in their faces. "I mean, with so many advances in medicine and mental health issues maybe a miracle will happen?"

"Well, I'm glad you still believe in miracles," answered Grant. "But I'm afraid there is absolutely no expectation of any significant advances, at least not in Kevin's lifetime."

"Well, you know that the Boston Latin School offers so many cool options," Sam said. "I'm taking one of them – a fact-checking and research course. It's a credit program that takes six weeks to complete and I thought it would be interesting. The other option was music appreciation, but I really don't want to appreciate my music other than by listening to it. So I think I'll do a little investigation into birth defects as one of the two projects that I have to do."

"That's a great idea on several levels," said Grant as he reached over to pat Sam's arm. "Maybe you'll find that miracle we all wish for. As well, research and accurate analysis is a major component in business and other projects. And making sure that the facts are right can mean the difference between a big win and looking like a twit. Certainly in the law enforcement field it's a critical factor."

"I'm glad you agree with me Dad," said Sam. "Of course, I'm still waiting, after five years, with eager anticipation to hear at least some of the stories about your crime fighting exploits that you promised to share with me...which you haven't. Got something to hide?"

Grant couldn't hold back his own laughter when he looked at his son trying to put an evil grin on his face and not succeeding very well. As a young man, Grant had dreamed of changing the world, making it free of crime and brutality. During his active service in law enforcement in Canada, he had risen in the ranks to an RCMP Inspector earlier than most. He was often in the forefront of raids and undercover operations, leading his team rather than directing them. He had an uncanny ability to spot fear and weakness in others making him very effective against the criminals he faced every day.

An intensely private man, he rarely spoke of his childhood and troubled early life. He was a man of few words and even fewer social graces who wouldn't tolerate incompetence or corruption in any of his colleagues. His contempt for political expediency was well known, and he had never tailored an investigation to suit the powers that be.

"Is that really true?" asked Grant with a sheepish grin, "that I haven't told you all about the brave and brilliant exploits of your very own father? I must have been drinking."

"Ha, you wish," said Sam. "But I'll tell you something very surprising that I have learned during this course. The instructor keeps emphasizing that the internet is often not a reliable source. One has to check books, or documented events and dates – even the actual given names of individuals. I always thought the internet was like the written word from above, and, in the couple of specific assignments Rhonda and I had to do, it turned out that some of the information taken from the internet was wrong."

"Rhonda?" asked Grant as he turned to Sam with his own Cheshire grin. "Who is Rhonda?"

"Just a classmate," answered Sam turning to look out the window, knowing that his face was now beet red. "She and I were assigned to work as a team on our first project, 'Blood Libel,' by Mr. Hazelton. She is actually pretty smart."

"And what about her looks?" asked Grant, feeling suddenly older. "Is she worthy of my son?"

Now it was Sam's turn to have some fun. "Looks?" he bellowed to his father. "What does that mean? Are you a sexist? Is it only about looks? I am just about to become a real life teenager. You have to be careful what you say to me. I could be traumatized. But, yah, she is a real looker."

Grant burst out laughing again. "You're the best Sam," he said. "I'm so lucky to be your father."

It was close to five o'clock when father and son turned into the long driveway leading up to the Home. When they got out of the car and started walking towards the front entrance they heard Kevin's voice calling to them. They turned as he came running from the playground off to the left. Almost six feet tall and weighing close to 165 pounds, Kevin Teasdale would, in another time and place, be seen as a handsome hunk. But when he spoke and when you looked into his eyes, his disability became apparent.

"Daddy, Daddy, look what I can do with the new iPad you and Sammy gave me for my birthday!" he shouted with obvious delight. "I can paint real pictures!"

Kevin embraced his father making sure to hold his iPad aloft and then lifted his brother Sam up in the air and spun him around.

"Sammy, what do you think I should try next?" he asked as he put Sam back on the ground. "Should I make a song?"

Kevin was jumping and laughing. "I read some of the words in the booklet and maybe I can figure out how to make a record of me singing. Will you show me for sure how to do it? Please, please?"

"Do you want to stop at The Cheesecake Factory for a bite?" asked Grant as he and Sam drove north on I-95 towards home. It was after seven o'clock and Grant was hungry. They had said goodbye to a very excited Kevin who could barely lift his head from the iPad that was now recording his voice – thanks to the instructions given by his younger brother – and for Grant it had been one of those priceless moments. He was still feeling the overwhelming love between his boys as he had watched Sam explain and show Kevin how to use his iPad as carefully and as simply as it could be done.

I am blessed, he thought as he enjoyed both his cappuccino and watching Sam attack his chocolate chip cheesecake. *How I wish I could verbalize my feelings to my sons. They have both given my life its meaning. I hope that they know how much they are loved.*

Grant knew that it was soon going to be the right time to begin the process of telling Sam about his heritage – good stuff and not such good stuff.

Grant and Lisa had started tossing the subject of Sam's heritage around, specifically the activities of his late grandmother Rebecca, during their last face to face get together in Boston at Christmas. Over the years the two of them had monthly "from the heart" conversations by telephone about their hopes for Sam's future, their own activities, and the up to date gossip about the DeLuca/Brattini families – in a limited way. Grant didn't like to use the internet.

Lisa had always told Sam that even though his Mom and Dad weren't married, they were still "best buddies" sharing his life in friendship and with lots of good humour. She had made the circumstances of Sam's birth work for all of them – especially Sam. She and Grant maintained a comfort level with each other that made it so easy for all their friends and family. Whenever Lisa came to Florida on a photo shoot that was near Grant's houseboat, she stayed there. And there was a permanent guest room in Lisa's home for Grant during his frequent visits to Boston.

Sam's conception had never been referred to as a "drunken one-nighter," but his parents didn't romanticize it either. They just didn't want to lie to him and were as honest about it as they felt they could be without causing him any unnecessary pain.

Grant attended every school event, sports event and any other special event that was important to Sam, often flying up to Boston and back to Florida on the same day. Over the years Grant and Lisa often spoke to Sam about his late grandmother, Rebecca, and her friendship with both Nonna Elizabeth and her late husband, Santino. It had always been during casual conversations and Sam had really never been that interested – the latest video games, his iPad and trying to beat his father at golf were more important to him. Sam was being raised in the Jewish religion, but his father's Catholic heritage played a large role in his life. He spent Christmas and Easter with Grant and enjoyed going to Church with him – though he did not actively participate. His parents had not yet defined when and the way in which they would tell Sam about his heritage.

They'd had their first conversation about it when Grant had first learned of Sam's birth. It was the first day of the new millennium; a cold, snowy Boston morning in the music room of Elizabeth DeLuca's home. Grant had stayed over once he saw Sam and realized that the drunken "event" had resulted in the birth of his son.

Lisa Sherman was the spitting image of her late father, Steve. She had auburn hair that curled around her face, her saucer-like brown eyes were always sparkling, and when she laughed her huge dimples were a delight. She liked to refer to herself as Rubenesque when describing her figure as compared to the thin models she photographed. She was a very successful commercial photographer and her pictures graced the covers of many international magazines. Lisa did what Lisa wanted, occasionally listening to the advice of others but rarely following it. Grant always smiled when he thought about her, and he remembered their conversation that day with such clarity.

I sat down next to Lisa and put my arm around her.

"I want to marry you," I said, smiling at her. "Sam is my son. Though his conception wasn't the optimum, I would be thrilled and honoured to have both of you in my life. And Lisa, I know that your mother, wherever she may be, is schlepping nachos over this."

Lisa burst out laughing. "You've mixed up Yiddish with Spanish!" she howled at me, clutching her stomach as she laughed. "It's shepping nachas, which is a traditional Jewish expression – it is kvelling, which means pleasure – deep down, next to the heart pleasure. What you just said means to drag nachos."

I put my hand over my eyes. You moron – how could you be so stupid?

"So why are you trying to speak Yiddish when you are a flaming red-haired goy!" she continued, still laughing.

"Well, I did pick up some expressions from your mother over the years and I guess I mixed them up," I answered sheepishly.

Lisa kept bursting into giggles every time she tried to continue our conversation. Finally she took some deep breaths and tried to stop laughing. But when she took my hand she burst out laughing again.

"Okay, now I have to settle down," she said in a serious voice. "I have lots to tell you." She took several deep breaths, stifled a few more giggles and began to share the last two years of her life with him.

"I have a wonderful partner who has been helping me to stop blaming myself about what happened," she began, almost in a whisper. "I was pretty much on my own as a teenager, and I thought I must have been a disappointment to my mother. She was always on a project that took all her waking hours; she barely noticed me and never asked about anything I was doing. Who knows how or where I would have ended up if not for my father who was really my best friend.

"And then, when I married that idiot Jeff who kept beating up on me because he couldn't get it up because it turned out that he went both ways, it was really icing on the cake."

I felt the blood rushing to my face as I envisioned myself pounding out both the senator and his nephew.

"My photography career helped me get through the night," she went on. "And to answer your unspoken question, no, I never wanted to share any of what happened to me with my mother. Who knows what she might have done, all in the name of settling a score."

"Then there was you," she went on, smiling at him. "I don't know why we did it. It certainly wasn't anything I had planned or had even thought about. But when Sam was born I was ecstatic. And while I was in the hospital I met a doctor who became my shoulder to lean on... and my lover. Her name is Isobel and we are partners."

"I hope your choice of partner didn't happen because I was so lousy in bed," I blurted out, instantly wishing I had kept my mouth shut.

But Lisa just threw back her head and laughed again. "You guys, you're all the same! You can only think with the lower half of your body and rarely does your brain function north of your waist."

Well, that tells me off appropriately. Now keep your mouth shut!

"Anyhow, as I said, I was thrilled about the pregnancy," continued Lisa. "Elizabeth stepped in right away and moved me into her Boston home. She announced that she would be the 'bubbie' that my baby had to have – only she would be an Italian bubbie, known as Nonna. She is so very special.

"I took her advice and didn't sell the Tranby property in Toronto. But it's rented out so I have some income.

"Elizabeth and I have had some very from the heart conversations," Lisa continued. "She told me about Santino and Mom. I already knew something had been going on between them, but not in the details that Elizabeth shared with me."

I am sure there were some details that Elizabeth left out, I thought, watching Lisa's face as she spoke.

"Elizabeth also told me about her promise to my mother to look after me, which I was happy to let her do, initially.

"It was nice to learn that my mother was concerned about me at the end," Lisa continued. "Though I'm not sure how much she thought of me in the early years. But with Elizabeth I felt safe putting myself in someone else's hands.

"She knows about Isobel and welcomed her and encouraged me to live as I choose to live.

"Isobel and I are ready to start a life together," Lisa went on emphatically. "But I will not do anything unless you approve. Sam is your son and I am so proud that he is. One day I would like you to tell us both about your relationship with my mother – his grandmother – but I understand that you will need to think about all of this for a while before you're ready.

"I want your blessings and your confidence that Sam's best interests are what count for me as I know they do for you. You will have unlimited access to him. I know you are living in Florida and I'm sure he will love to visit you there.

"I am going to continue to live in Boston," Lisa went on. "My business is doing well and I don't want to start all over again. You are listed on Sam's birth certificate as his father – his official last name is Teasdale. I am still a Canadian and so are you; so he has dual citizenship."

I had said nothing during Lisa's monologue, but I know she saw the tears I was trying to hide.

"You're very quiet Grant. Is there anything you would like to say before I continue?"

I was overwhelmed with emotions and it took me a few minutes to find the right words to say.

"Lisa, how lucky Sam will be all of his life to have you as his mother. I welcome him into my life and I welcome you as well, wherever I am and wherever I may go. I expect to stay in Florida. He will know that he has parents who love him and respect each other. Hopefully that will make his journey through life successful.

"And now, to quote my beloved Rebecca, let's talk about the money. I intend to provide you both with all the financial support you will ever need, or want."

We continued talking until the early afternoon. There were no contentious issues between us, and I assured her that I had no concerns about her lifestyle or that it would have a negative effect on Sam. After living a brutal childhood in an orphanage myself, I knew that nothing can hurt a child who is surrounded by love – love from family – whatever their choices.

We were in total agreement on how to proceed for the next fifty years with only one subject to be left open until both of us felt the time was right. And that was when and how to tell Sam about his heritage.

"Maybe if I had understood what drove my mother perhaps I would have made better choices for myself," said Lisa as she put her arms around my shoulders and we held each other.

"And in today's world of instant information there are no more secrets. So it's better for Sam to learn it all, the good and the bad, from us, rather than from the internet or some other source. Let's give ourselves ten years before we have to think about it again."

CHAPTER TWO

Cornwall, Ontario.

It was winter and, on this particular night, the undercover agents on assignment were members from the FBI and INSETs (Integrated National Security Enforcement Teams). They had arrived in Cornwall around midnight and saw that the Mohawk men had parked their Escalade outside a tavern located off Pitt Street, near the main highway. When the team pulled into the parking lot, they backed up their truck to face both the SUV and the road.

Their assignment was simply to follow the money – to watch and record the smugglers' network of contacts, safe houses and hopefully, once over the border, the money launderers. Although the assignment was straightforward, the Canadian–American politics leading up to this investigation was anything but.

For many years Canada was known as the place to go to hide in plain sight. There were close to 100,000 illegal Arabs in Quebec, primarily Montreal – mostly Lebanese, Syrians and Somalis. In Kamloops, British Columbia, a recent arrest of some Palestinians trying to sneak across the border into the United States raised another red flag about security breaches at the border. And the question of how those Palestinians even got into Canada in the first place has yet to be answered.

The former Canadian Liberal government kept falling over itself trying to appease their left-wing supporters by sucking up to the United Nations despots, so most of the beneficiaries of Canada's largesse were those from the Middle East with deep loyalties to countries that harboured terrorists. The bureaucrats were also very powerful, too powerful according to the US intelligence service, which viewed the lax Canadian immigration policies, developed and implemented by the Francophones, as a real concern.

But with the recent election of a majority Conservative government, the United States was now ready to work more closely with their neighbours to the north, and they were happy about it. This prime minister could be counted on to honour his commitments and to support his country's closest ally in its efforts to seek out and destroy any group that posed a threat to both their interests. He was also committed to clamping down on the previous government's immigration loopholes, which allowed too many drug lords, corrupt Middle Eastern politicians and Soviet gangsters to slip into Canada and, once there, deposit drug money and transfer assets, usually stolen, into Canadian banks.

The Russians had made serious inroads into the crime business in North America – once the purview of the Italians and the Chinese. Rumours had recently surfaced that they were branching out, incredibly, by enlisting the help of some of the First Nations. Due to the Jay Treaty of 1794 between the United States and Great Britain, the Mohawk had the right to pass between the Canada–US border freely with no checks, and for some it was a smuggler's dream. There was nothing both governments could do about it short of rescinding the Treaty, which was impossible. Canada had been notorious for its leniency when it came to its aboriginal population anyhow – guilt over past abuses, no doubt, but still a reality and crime bosses knew it.

Eastern European organized crime groups were using aboriginal lands to transport drugs, cigarettes and people using riverfront property along the St. Lawrence River into the Cornwall area. A group of the Mohawk people were now demanding their share of the action. Even the Mexicans and Chinese had started to quietly recruit their own "aboriginal force," as they liked to call them, and the US government was not happy about it.

The general disinterest by Canadian Parliament of aboriginal affairs allowed corrupt government officials, under the guise of Indian Affairs, to divert millions of dollars into their pockets and those of their friends. Many aboriginal communities had been given a major stake in oil, gas, mining and lumber developments through the land given back to them by the government – not in real time, but as the front for those appointed to manage and oversee their operations.

Those appointees never shared their winnings with the people they were supposed to be helping. The issue was not as blatant in the United States as it was in Canada, but given their shared border and the sensitive technological information that could be leaked to whoever was prepared to pay the most, the United States began to take a deeper look at what was actually going on in the companies they believed were a front for governments not friendly to them.

So the fact that the new crime bosses – Italian, Chinese and especially the Russians – were using First Nations and specifically the Mohawk as couriers was known to very few outside the FBI and INSET. Both agencies were anxious to keep it that way until they could crack into the Mob's operations.

The lead on this project was a woman known only as Sally. Her real name was Jennifer White. She decided it was time to rattle the prey's cages. Wearing a black ski mask that left only her eyes visible, she got out of the truck and quickly moved like a small iguana along the dirt path over to the Escalade.

That Cadillac has to belong to someone a step or two up the ladder, she thought. *Couriers use second-hand vans or trucks.*

Once she reached the SUV and saw that it wasn't armoured, she quickly opened the hood and planted a small explosive device by the ignition; she was excited to see what would happen when it blew and how the smugglers would react. Even though there was no official plan to intervene and no way to stop them from crossing the border into the United States with the money, Jennie had the authority to use her discretion and judgement. She thought that a diversion such as this might net the agents some useful information. She was back in the truck within five minutes.

The door to the tavern opened minutes later and out came three men, obviously drunk. Two got in the back of the SUV, the other took a gym bag out of the trunk, opened the driver's door and heaved it onto the front seat as he climbed in after it. From the way he had to shove it up and in with his shoulder, the agents knew the bag was full.

As the man slammed his door shut, the entire SUV exploded. The agents initially froze – then started their truck and took off.

"Wait! Stop!" yelled Jennie. "That SUV had to have been wired before we got here. My explosive was a glorified firecracker. Someone set these guys up, and I want to see what I can get from that car before it is total ashes."

They spun the truck around and Jennie jumped out and ran in a crouch to the burning SUV. She went around to the driver's side, which was already crumbling under the heat. She shot through the door and then pulled it so hard it came off the hinge. Cringing at the sight of the driver immersed in flames, she grabbed what was left of the gym bag next to him and threw it on the ground. She felt the weight.

The other agents had broken open the back door and managed to pull out the other two men; both were burned horribly – one was obviously dead, but one was still moaning.

"Grab him, put him in our truck!" yelled Jennie. "We'll take him back to the field office."

Still there were no sirens, no one visible around the tavern. It was as though what had just happened hadn't happened at all – that it was expected and no one wanted to be around as a witness. Jennie guessed that the explosive was set off by someone watching the SUV but who couldn't see the agents nearby. Or it was a remote on a timer.

Jennie sat inside the truck holding the burned Mohawk and pulled out the emergency kit from under the seat as they took off. She found a small tube of Polysporin in the emergency pack – good for minor finger burns, but it was all she had. The man was trying to speak. Jennie was always wired when she was on assignment, so she put her chest and the attached microphone against the man's face to record anything he said as she tried to soothe him. He spoke a language unfamiliar to Jenny for about a minute, and then he turned his head and died. Jennie had no idea what he said, nor could she remember ever hearing that First Nations dialect before.

The gym bag was in tatters, but what was still left inside appeared to be a huge sack of coloured stones. At first, Jennie missed the diamonds hidden at the bottom next to a rubber pouch that looked like the ones used for their interoffice memos; it was also in tatters. Jennie was pretty sure there could not have been much money in the bag. Millions of dollars, even in large bills, could not have been completely obliterated in such a short time – but heroin or methamphetamine would have. The remnants of foil wrapping reinforced her assessment.

"Well, I guess I'm going to have a lot of explaining to do," whispered Jennie to her colleagues.

They nodded and grunted.

"The good news is that if we hadn't planned our little operation, we would have missed the diamonds, and the explosion would have gone unnoticed, at least to us, for some time. The bad news is that we have nothing else to show...yet. Just a little rubber pouch – let's hope there's some good stuff inside it."

Inside that rubber pouch was a scrap of paper – what was left of a memo that had an Israeli foreign ministry stamp and words that were now barely legible: "P&M, Latchman & Howard Ramsay" as well as words that looked like "The 3rd hole."

CHAPTER THREE

Pt. St. Lucie, Florida.

Later that night, after Sam was asleep, Grant went into his office and walked over to the wall safe hidden just above the floor behind a large loveseat – not a usual hiding spot, but at the time he did it Grant thought it was a good idea. But now as he had to get on his knees to open the safe, he laughed at his "once brilliant idea."

When he had the files next to him, he sat down on the love seat and stretched out, lifting his legs onto the ottoman. He closed his eyes and was instantly back in time – the pain overwhelmed him, again.

Twenty years earlier he had been seconded to the head of a joint FBI–RCMP task force investigating the Mafia – focussing on the Villano crime family and its boss, Santino DeLuca. They had been making a fortune on their US gambling operations and then laundering the money in Canada to avoid paying taxes by delivering millions of dollars in cash to various Canadian banks that, so far, had refused to cooperate. Finally, under pressure from his US counterpart, the Minister of Justice agreed that the IRS would be allowed to work in partnership with the joint task force to do a Canadian version of the famous "Al Capone exercise," and try to nail the moneybags on tax evasion.

It was this investigation that first brought Grant into contact with Rebecca Sherman – rumoured to be the DeLuca's right hand and also his lover. She had controlled his multi-million dollar investment fund, the P&M Trust; almost tripling its value over a fifteen-year period. The only name to appear on any of the Trust's documents was Sherman's because of the banking laws of those countries where she had invested the capital. Rebecca Sherman was simply a front for a fund being administered under her sole control thus ensuring that the DeLuca name never came into play. As a result, the Trust was protected from any "probable cause" that might have become applicable when the FBI expanded its investigation into DeLuca's activities.

During the investigation, the FBI could not find any evidence that this fund was being used to launder drug money. They knew that Rebecca Sherman had transferred a large sum of money to a company that was incorporated in Tel Aviv. As a Diaspora Jew, she was entitled to certain protection not afforded to non-Jews. The Israeli government was encouraging its people to return to their roots, and they were offering some very special privileges using the protection of assets as an incentive. The origin of the money was never discovered during the investigation, and Israel was not cooperative with the FBI, so no charges could be made.

The FBI informants' reports on Sherman's activities and Teasdale's own assessment showed her to be shrewd, ruthless and amoral. Despite the lengthy file on her, there was nothing that gave them enough to crack her silence.

Even knowing the risks, Teasdale had found himself taking more than a professional interest in Rebecca Sherman. At first he rationalized that he was just "working undercover" – after all, she was older than him, but he knew that he was only kidding himself. There had been an instant chemistry between them that was very hard to ignore. He did try. He knew that he wasn't handling her case in as detached and professional way as he should. When his concern for Rebecca Sherman had approached a danger zone he convinced himself that he had better back off – and fast.

During the year of the investigation he kept his distance, but when it was over and she had served prison time, when she had left DeLuca

Enterprises, when DeLuca had died, they had bumped into each other in Boston the night before DeLuca's memorial and all bets were off.

We were still chatting away when we reached her room. Once inside, I grabbed her and we kissed and kissed, nibbling on each other's lips and tongues. She made no sounds as she kept her arms wrapped around my neck while I kept kissing and holding her close. Suddenly she pushed me back, stared intently into my eyes for what seemed like a long time and then lifted her sweater over her head.

I burst out laughing – I couldn't help myself. Her eyes never left mine. "You're not the boss here Mrs. Sherman," I whispered. "I am."

I pulled her back to the bed, unhooked her bra, sat down as she was still standing in front of me and ran my hands up to her already hard nipples. I sucked on them while I put my hands inside her skirt's waistband and pulled it off along with her underwear. She had already spread her legs when I slipped first one, then another finger inside her. When I ran my thumb along her my fingers rotated inside her. She let out a cry and continued to moan as she pushed my shoulders back until I was half lying on the bed. She unhooked my belt.

"Can't I be the boss for just a little while?" she asked me, half smiling as her hand slipped inside my pants and she cupped my balls before she sank to her knees and ran her tongue along the tip of my penis.

Oh shit. I am about to lose it, I thought as I pulled her down on top of me and then flipped her over. I could only get my pants half way down before I lunged inside her and, despite my best efforts, had an immediate orgasm. I let out a groan that combined pleasure and frustration at how fast it had all happened.

"Say the wrong thing, and we could have a major issue here," I said, ignoring her giggles as I kept holding her in my arms.

"Oh boy," she laughed as she turned over and yawned. "Do you ever have to do lots of yummy things to me to make up for this quick exercise."

I will never be without you again, I thought as I wrapped my arms around her and dozed off.

Along with the files from the DeLuca investigation, Grant held in his hand documents that he obtained after Rebecca died. Peter DeLuca and his associate Yuri Latchman had given them to Rebecca a week before she was killed. They contained evidence that implicated a number of high-profile politicians and power brokers, Canada's Deputy Minister of Justice Howard Ramsay among them. Knowing the implications these documents could have should they ever be discovered and made public, Grant believed they were the reason she was killed. His gut told him Yuri Latchman helped to make that happen, but no matter how long Grant looked over his files, he couldn't prove it.

It is time to put this all away, he thought as he looked at documents and files. *Sam needs a father who is in the moment, not someone with his heart still in the past. Move on!*

Grant picked up the papers and put them back into the safe. Then he went into Sam's room and smiled at his sleeping face.

You're mine – and I love you.

CHAPTER FOUR

Palm Beach, Florida.

Peter DeLuca was sipping iced tea at his regular table at Carlos and Charlie's Bistro as he waited for Yuri Latchman. Tall and thin, his green eyes were on the move as he glanced at those around him and those walking along the sidewalk. He always enjoyed the sights and sounds of this bustling neighbourhood. The spitting image of his mother, Peter was dressed in Armani, as usual.

He was very pragmatic, a realist. He approached all situations head-on, prepared for confrontation. Even as a little boy, he would sit down, think through a problem and come up with the best strategy to obtain the result he desired. But his quick temper made it just as likely that he would lash out when provoked rather than react calmly. He was also very protective of his brother Matthew, his fraternal twin.

Matthew was a priest who worked directly with the Vatican on political and financial matters. An idealist who still believed in the principles of social justice and equality, he was a gentle giant who loved to read mystery novels and listen to classical music. His decision to become a priest was shaped by two realities – trying to make up for his late father's criminal activities and…his love for Angela Brattini. After graduating from Harvard, Matthew gave up on getting over Angela, moving on with his life and finding someone else. He just turned to the Church which offered him the peace he wanted and the opportunity to pay penance for the heritage his father, whom he loved dearly, had left him and Peter.

Sitting next to Peter at the table was Lenny Brattuso, friend, aide and financial wizard who was the comptroller of DeLuca Industries. Lenny was a carbon copy of his late father Vinnie, who had been one of Santino DeLuca's most trusted men. Lenny was responsible for bringing the legitimate holdings of DeLuca Industries into the modern day world – a world of high-tech, the IRS and the RICO statute.

Over the years, Peter had gone through his own *Voyage of the Damned*, never knowing how much his last visit with Rebecca Sherman and the evidence he and Latchman had given her on Ramsay and others had contributed to the chain of events that led to her murder. He was surprised at how much remorse he felt despite Latchman's insistence that neither one of them had any responsibility for what had happened. Peter was convinced that Yuri never felt guilty about anything, ever, so he took his assurances rather lightly.

Peter's mother's close involvement with Rebecca's daughter Lisa and her son Sam didn't help. Elizabeth was devoted to both of them and her role as Sam's Italian bubbie also didn't help. Though he knew that his late father and Rebecca had been lovers and that Rebecca had played a key role in the financial success of the P&M Trust, he knew that there were still parts of that puzzle to be uncovered, especially where the money had disappeared to. His wife Angela, whom he adored and to whom he had been married for ten years, was constantly encouraging him to let the past fade away.

"Think about our girls," she often said. "There is a whole new world of options available to them – options that were never available to your mother. Let them fly Peter; they need to be free. You have to put the past in a jar and throw it out to sea."

Angela had managed to do just that – never looking back at the reality of her own birth – but that reality was an ongoing aspect in their lives. Like her mother-in-law Elizabeth's violent heritage, it had put them all on the path that brought them to the present...and to the problems that had to be dealt with.

"Hi Peter," said Yuri Latchman with a smile as he took off his sun glasses and sat down. "And you too Lenny." Brattuso nodded without expression.

Latchman was built like a bulldog and looked like a boxer. Five foot ten, shoulders and arms like rocks, dark brown eyes and almost no hair. He was vicious and vindictive and though Peter had several projects in which Yuri had a piece, he was never comfortable with him.

Latchman was born in Magadan, Russia, a city in the old Siberian gulag with a grim history – rumour had it that the main highway contained the bones of the peasants who had been forced to build it. He had no memory of his father who disappeared before Yuri was born. His mother believed that he had gone to America but there was no record of it. His father's brother, Boris, was his surrogate father and in whatever limited capacity Yuri had to love anyone, he loved Boris who had arrived in the United States and then into Canada through Israel. Many Russian mobsters wanting to leave the Soviet Union claimed to be Jewish because it made their access into Israel a given which then made their entry to the United States and Canada easier. Once in the country they changed their names, making it harder to trace their roots.

But Yuri's uncle and surrogate father, the late Boris Latchman, was Jewish. Very little was known about Boris Latchman other than he had, or could get, large amounts of cash, no questions asked.

He had once owned Bayfield Trust and had been the money man to see twenty years earlier when Santino DeLuca was looking to expand his interests and needed cash. His associate Bob DeSalle had set up a meeting between the two men. Boris had been impressed with Santino DeLuca and bought all the outstanding bank loans of the P&M Trust for six million dollars. He also agreed to extend a further three million dollars in credit to DeLuca on his personal guarantee. Bob DeSalle received a finder's fee of one hundred thousand dollars.

Yuri Latchman looked around the patio and out to the street. "Great spot to check out all the action," he said to Peter as he handed him a small package. "Sorry I couldn't get back in time for your birthday party, but I couldn't get a flight out of Belgrade in time to make the right connection. I figured this gift would make up for it."

Peter removed the wrapping from the package and inside was a small tissue paper packet containing an exquisite diamond, uncut, but still spectacular. Ten carats. Peter let out a big whistle.

"This is a bit too much Yuri," he said as he rewrapped the gem. "Were you and I planning to get engaged? Are you giving me this in lieu of a ring?"

Both Lenny and Yuri burst out laughing. When the waiter approached to take his order, Yuri asked for the lobster bisque and vodka on ice.

"Hah, that's really funny Peter," he answered. "It's part of the merchandise we are importing from Minsk."

"Well, I need the right documentation beforehand," said Lenny. "So whenever you're ready, we need to sit down and work it all out."

"Man, are you always doing business?" asked Yuri as Lenny examined the diamond. "Don't you ever cut loose? Have a few laughs? Get a blow job from a nice lady of the night?"

"The answer is yes!" laughed Lenny, still turning the diamond in his hand. "But business is business, anytime, anyplace."

The three men spent the rest of the afternoon discussing business, namely how to transport and import through legitimate means all the "goods and services" that Latchman's enterprises controlled. They talked about documentation, accounting, marked down inventory costs and major under-evaluation of merchandise for tax purposes.

Peter reiterated that any and all drug importing had to go through Latchman's east European operations. "We will not do drugs under any circumstances," said Peter emphatically. "We only do diamonds. We'll also launder whatever money you need to hide for a twenty percent piece of the gross amount."

"What?" yelled Yuri, almost spilling his soup. "Nobody gets that kind of action. There are plenty of cleaners around who will do it for a lot less."

"We aren't like anybody else," Lenny quietly interjected. "And you know it. With us you can be sure there will be no ugly surprises, no paper trails carelessly left behind and no risk to you or your people."

"And again Yuri," Peter said forcefully, "there will be no drugs brought in through any of our companies or any of the merchandise we will be importing through you. If I get one sniff that you are trying to pull a fast one, look out!"

"You know Peter, with all due respect," said Latchman with a laugh. "I think you are just deluding yourself. Not touching something with your own hands doesn't mean you can't get dirty just the same as the rest of us mere mortals.

"If you are so opposed to the drug trade," he went on, minus the smile, "get out of this business altogether. There is nothing that happens in the world in which we travel that doesn't have something to do with it, directly or indirectly."

Neither DeLuca nor Lenny Brattuso said a word.

"However, I will go along with your little charade," Yuri continued. "Nothing that can even be thought of as a drug will come near DeLuca Industries. You have my promise."

CHAPTER FIVE

Washington, D.C. FBI Headquarters.

Bob Lantinos, number two at the FBI, was in the director's office to meet with Jake Bartoli, former CIA operative in Serbia and now one of the president's senior advisors. Lantinos was a fitness freak and was built like a five-foot-eight boxer. His black curly hair was always falling into his eyes – he had no time, so he said, for regular visits to the barber shop. He was the son of Greek immigrants who had made it into the United States just one week before he was born. Bob had made his mother so happy when he had married Olivia Theos, the daughter of one of her best friends – so happy that she stopped nagging him about changing his profession.

"Why do you have to carry a gun?" she used to ask him, again and again. "You went to Harvard. Why can't you be a lawyer?"

Bob and Olivia had a good marriage – they had two sons, both now living in California, and a grandchild was on the way. Olivia was beside herself with excitement.

Jake Bartoli was an old friend of Lantinos and of Grant Teasdale with whom he had worked on the Villano crime family investigations several years earlier. Jake was a little person, barely over four feet tall, but he had his black belt which levelled the playing field for him.

"Homeland Security has alerted us to a concern about a very senior Canadian bureaucrat," said Jake. "Howard Ramsay, the Deputy Minister of Justice in the federal government. He's the former Justice of the Ontario Court of Appeals, and now one of the most prominent Canadian power brokers representing First Nations interests."

"I know him," replied Lantinos. "He was under investigation years ago in connection with possible payoffs from the Mafia, but no useable evidence was ever found."

Lantinos also knew from the FBI's own investigation that Ramsay was somehow involved in the smuggling ring out of Cornwall. But he let Bartoli continue, intrigued that the presidential advisor was gathering similar information as the FBI.

"Right," said Jake. "He was also a board member of the Federal Bridge Corporation, which governed several Border crossings between New York State and the Province of Ontario. This concerned the US Department of Justice. They wanted to make sure that the interests of both countries continued to be compatible.

"And we are asking the FBI to have a look – specifically at the activities of the Deputy Minister of Justice, Howard Ramsay. He has access to confidential communications between the president and the new prime minister."

"This doesn't sound important enough to involve the White House," said Lantinos. "What's the real scoop?"

"The Russians," answered Bartoli. "The CIA has had several tips about the Russians planning a direct underground smuggling route from Ontario to New York. They would have to use someone with aboriginal status – they're the only ones allowed to cross borders without any inspection. A name mentioned several times is Yuri Latchman, a known associate of Peter DeLuca, son of the late head of the Villano crime family."

"Oh, I know about them," interjected Lantinos with spiked interest. Lantinos thought again about the evidence from Cornwall – the memo read "P&M Latchman & Howard Ramsay." The P&M Fund had been run by Rebecca Sherman but owned by Peter DeLuca's late father, Santino DeLuca. "I didn't realize Peter DeLuca was following in his father's bloody footprints."

"Well, not exactly," said Bartoli. "This DeLuca is also a Harvard graduate who has used his skills in finance to camouflage any illegal activities of DeLuca Industries the way his father never could. We are still working on it.

"One of the aboriginal names connected to Ramsay and by implication, Latchman, is Julius Manon, the chief of a band in Lillooet, British Columbia," Bartoli continued. "Five years ago he was involved in several bombings leading into the reservation there. He has also made comments, recorded, about doing a 9/11 to lift the plight of aboriginals to the top of the government's agenda. Last week four Palestinians were arrested in Kamloops, BC, trying to get into the US. They had no papers except a piece of one with a telephone number – Julius Manon. And of course the question of how they got into Canada in the first place needs to be answered…and not by us.

"Despite Manon's attempts to rationalize his violent acts with pontifications of caring about the plight of his people," Bartoli continued, "he was caught in a takedown in Seattle last year. Drugs…and explosive materials, which brought in Homeland Security, and eventually brought in me.

"With evidence of a connection between Ramsay and Latchman, and Ramsay and Chief Manon, there is a genuine concern about Canada's unofficial role in this situation.

"Last week the president spoke to the prime minister on a one-to-one basis at the G8 finance meeting in Washington," Bartoli continued. "He expressed the need for absolute confidentiality between the two of them. When the prime minister agreed, the president decided to take a chance and tell him about his hesitations, specifically regarding Howard Ramsay. It turns out that the current prime minister has the same concerns. He had heard the rumours about a former prime minister who was taking bribes from the same mobsters out of Montreal…and Ramsay was the middle man for the payoffs."

"I hear what you are saying," said Lantinos. "But still, this isn't that big a deal to involve the CIA and the White House. Sounds like the usual crooks and corrupt politicians. So what have you left out and what else is new?"

"What else is new is Yuri Latchman's uncle's former ties to Boris Yeltsin – information that we have just uncovered," answered Bartoli.

"It was Latchman's underground diamond smuggling operation that funded Yeltsin until 1992 when the privatization of state assets, particularly in the oil, gas and minerals, a.k.a. diamond sectors, took over after the Soviet Union's collapse.

"Five years ago Yuri Latchman took over what was left of the business and expanded it," Jake went on, "but this time the primary beneficiary was the new president. Wouldn't it be a wonderful bonus for the United States if we could get some documented proof? It could do wonders for the Russian people.

"We know that Latchman is also tied in with DeLuca though we haven't yet been able to nail them definitively," Bartoli continued. "Peter DeLuca is the Mob – and his wife is the sister of Johnny Brattini, also the Mob. So the possibilities are wonderfully tantalizing. We want to let our best investigative team loose on this one – but not too loose.

"Bob, we need you to put the group together," Bartoli said. "Give them a name and then keep us informed. Nothing heavy, nothing documented – just who is who and what they are doing. Decisions on immunity or anything else are yours."

Lantinos couldn't help but be excited. Bartoli didn't know that the FBI was already investigating the smuggling ring between Canada and the United States. Bartoli's information helps explain the diamonds found by Jennifer White and the memo. Now with the president's support, Lantinos had justification to put more money and energy into the already active investigation.

"Of course," Bartoli continued, "involving Larry Lyons and hopefully his brother Grant Teasdale adds an even bigger carrot to this adventure. We are aware of their past personal involvements – Lyons, with DeLuca's widow Elizabeth, and Teasdale with the late Rebecca Sherman."

Lantinos didn't say anything for a few minutes. *No wonder you mentioned those two men specifically – no secrets are safe in today's world of high-tech.* But the possibilities of this kind of undercover investigation with a carte blanche agenda were impossible for Lantinos to refuse. On the other hand, he knew that he would not be able to share the specifics of this conversation with either brother. And after thirty years of a deep and loyal friendship, that felt like a betrayal on his part.

"Ok, let me talk to Larry about heading this joint investigation," said Lantinos, pushing away any twinges of guilt. "Most of the primary concerns are relative to Canadians – or action within their border. There is no doubt that Grant Teasdale will be available for anything Larry asks of him. But officially, this is better done with a Canadian in the lead and US investigators working alongside them. I already have an undercover agent in mind to work with them on this."

"Ok buddy, sounds good," said Jake as he reached up to shake Lantinos' hand. "No written reports – no documentation. We'll keep in touch about this face to face."

At the door he turned to Bob and chuckled, "This is almost like a Robert Ludlum novel – who do you think will play me in the movie?"

CHAPTER SIX

Juárez, Mexico.

Their timing was perfect. The white minivan in front of them suddenly swerved off the road and smashed into a large tree. They had been blindsided by one half of the FBI team – Jack Hoskins and Fred Ahmad who had been waiting in a small black Honda just off the side of the road. As the van approached, the Honda pulled out in front of them and started blaring its horn and flashing its lights.

When the other half of the team, agents Jennifer White and Dan Greenberg had begun chasing the van twenty miles back, whoever was inside didn't know who was following them. Rather than take any chances, they took off at very high speeds. In the bizarre world of Mexican and Colombian cartels, both of whom worked in and out of each other's countries, it was never clear who was the bait and who was the hunter. This group could be running from Mexican authorities or the enforcers of the Sinaloa cartel which operated quite openly in this part of Mexico. The favourite route of those trying to escape into the United States via El Paso was this one – Highway 45.

According to the Department of Justice, Mexican-based cartels were operating in more than one thousand US cities. And this FBI undercover unit, called the Gringos, ranked as number one internally, had begun intercepting shipments of cocaine, heat-sealed in one kilo bricks of Mylar foil. And the last package had been nabbed in New

Jersey. It was a given that the drugs passed through Massena, NY on the way to Jersey and the investigators needed to know if the point of origin was Cornwall, Ontario, or the El Paso, Texas, checkpoint.

As the agents ran to the van from different sides, guns drawn, the driver was trying to unbuckle himself. Jennie took a spark plug she kept in her pocket, often referred to as a ghetto glass breaker, and used it to smash the window. She reached in and grasped the driver's head, twisted it to the side and injected a tranquilizer into his neck with a small syringe. The guy in the passenger seat was no longer in it – he obviously hadn't been wearing a seat belt and his head, or what was left of it, was lying almost through the broken front window and on the hood of the car. On the floor in front of him was a large gym bag. Jennifer had trouble lifting it and tore open the zipper. There they were…again, a large bunch of coloured stones. She pushed the bag to the ground and spilled out the contents – at the bottom was a small black pouch filled with uncut diamonds.

What the fuck is going on? Second time in two busts? We're supposed to be following drugs and cash – something is going on that I don't know about.

In the meantime, Greenberg had slid back the other door and aimed his Taser at the two guys slumped in the seat. When they started to move he pulled the trigger, ejecting two barbed probes which embedded in their necks. A crackling pulse of electricity incapacitated them as he flex-cuffed their hands behind their backs. Then he took out a roll of duct tape and slapped a piece of each on their mouths.

Hoskins shot out the lock on the back door of the van and yanked it open. Sitting on the back seat was what looked like a makeshift catapult and several cartons marked sugar, a cover name used when shipping methamphetamine. Not only was meth addictive, it could be produced cheaply. It was often hidden, usually five kilos, in a five hundred pound stash of marijuana. Sitting next to the meth, gagged and bound, was a young boy, perhaps eight years old. Hoskins, who was fluent in Spanish, quickly lifted him out of the van and took him back to their car. At first he wouldn't answer Hoskins' questions about where he had come from, but once the kid saw Jennie he started to cry and call for his mother.

After the white van with the body inside was incinerated, the agents in two cars took off back down Highway 45. Jennifer was in the lead with Hoskins who was getting directions from the little boy leading them back to his house. He said that strange men had come with faces covered. They broke in the door and one of them had grabbed him and taken him out to the van and tied him up inside it before he went back to the house. His mother and father were in the house along with his two sisters. His name was Pedro, and he didn't know anything else.

There were no lights on as they turned up the dirt road towards a small wooden house sitting on a hill. Both vehicles stopped. The four agents got out to assess the situation and figure out their next move.

"There could be a shooter still inside," said Greenberg. "I mean, where is the kid's family? And who are they to warrant this kind of assault? The kid is dressed in glorified rags."

Hoskins was left to stay with Pedro and the other three put on ski masks and moved up to the house with Jennie in the lead and Greenberg and Ahmad on either side and slightly back.

The front door was hanging on its last hinge, having been kicked in by heavy boots. All three agents had their guns drawn as they crawled along the floor using their flashlights. Greenberg bumped into the first body with his knee before he actually saw him. A man, probably early thirties, shot in the chest. A few feet past him lay a woman, eyes staring blankly upward, her dress pulled up around her waist, her legs spread, and a coarse rope around her neck.

As Jenny came closer, she saw the bottom of a tequila bottle jutting out of her vagina. *Bastards. Wait until you start enjoying the funny things that your balls can do when they are being squeezed with a nice pair of pliers.*

Ahmad and Greenberg let out moans when they reached the tiny kitchen. They turned off their flashlights and turned away.

"Don't go in Jennie," said Ahmad.

She did and saw two little girls – no more than ten years old – naked on the floor, legs spread open, blood still wet on their legs and on the floor under them.

"Go get those guys," Jennie said in a very quiet voice. "Tell Hoskins to keep the kid in the car."

She sat down on the floor and tried to turn her feelings off – something she had done more than once in her career. *Why? What kind of pigs would do this?* But Jennie had seen it too often – and things that were even worse than this. Sometime during the last ten years she lost her sensitivity and was able to remain pretty detached. But when bad things happened to little kids, it was a kick in her gut and she could not let it go.

Then she heard a creaking sound near the back door. She flattened out hoping that the others would still be in attack mode. It was pitch black. She drew her Beretta and tossed her flashlight across the room hoping the noise would startle whoever was there. Suddenly a man's shadow appeared in the doorway and he fired. There was hardly any sound, but there was a flash visible in the darkness.

The shot ripped through the air over her head and hit the wall behind her. Before the man could get off a second shot, Jennie rose onto one knee and fired in the direction of the flash. She could hear the bullets from her gun tearing through the bones and flesh of a body that fell to the floor and was now moaning. She stood up and calmly walked over to him. He was staring up at her as she lifted her ski mask and spit in his face. Then she reached down, placed the gun barrel into his ear and fired. His body went still.

When Ahmad and Greenberg came running back inside it was all over.

"Bring them in," she said. "Don't untie them – just take their pants off."

"Now spread this one out and sit on his legs," she continued in an icy voice. "By the way, if either of you have any problems with what's coming, go and change places with Hoskins."

"I got no problem," said Ahmad. "I have a daughter."

All three smugglers were now awake; two were trussed up against the wall, naked from the waist down, eyes widened and trying not to look at their friend.

"By the way, these guys speak English," said Greenberg. "Hoskins spoke to them in Spanish, but they didn't respond. The kid said he heard them talking gringo."

Jennie walked over to her backpack and took out a large pair of pliers.

"Okay gentlemen, I only like to ask questions once," she said. "And we saw what you did to those two little girls."

"Who are you working for?"

A scream.

"I ask you again, who are you working for?"

A louder scream, lasting longer.

Ahmad and Greenberg kept their heads turned, but they didn't flinch or lighten up their hold on the guys' legs.

"Well, you still have one left that might function, so let me ask you for the third and last time. Who are you working for?"

The two other guys started yelling and crying. "Stop! Stop! We don't know – the Chief hired us!"

"The Chief?" howled Ahmad. "What the fuck is this? A cowboys and Indians movie?"

Jennie leaned over the man lying on the floor.

"Was it fun?" she asked, lighting a candle which she then used to heat one half of the pliers. "Shoving your cock into those little girls?"

"Yah, it was," the guy answered just as Jennie shoved the hot handle of the pliers up his ass. The screams continued even as Jennie pressed down hard on his hyoid bone on his neck. When it broke and his windpipe collapsed the screams ended. It was an unpleasant way to die.

The two other men started begging to be allowed to talk. It turned out that the guys were aboriginals – Mohawks from New York State. They spit out everything they knew. The dead man who'd shot at Jennie had been their leader. He had taken the boy to use him to smuggle their cache over the river – a diversionary tactic if necessary.

Take the kid onto the river, throw him in and make a lot of noise. When the police boats came to look for the kid, the smugglers were going to use the catapult to heave the stuff to the other side.

"Hey, that's not such a crazy story," said Ahmad. "I was reading the *New York Times* just last week and there was an article about using a catapult to fling hundred-pound bales of marijuana over the high-tech fence along a stretch of Arizona's border."

"Yah, but that's not a river," said Jennie.

"Well, the article talked about several ports of entries being used in the same way," he continued. "And there was a good quote about having the best fence that money can buy but being screwed by the twenty-five hundred-year-old technology of a catapult…or something like that."

The two Mohawk men kept babbling about an upcoming job. The Chief was meeting with the whole group soon, but they didn't know exactly when. And the Head Chief, who was the boss of their Chief, would be there. They didn't know his name, but one of them thought it was Rambone or Ram or something like that.

"Well, I have no problem wiping these guys out, considering what they did," said Jennifer. She was not kidding and her team knew it.

"No," said Ahmad. "Not now. We don't need any more heat on us or any more investigations. Turn them over to the Mexicans. Tell them they're snitches and should be locked up. That should do it."

Sadly for Pedro, he would also have to be turned over to the Mexican authorities, which was in itself cruel and unusual punishment. The team hoped he had some family out there who would take care of him.

Two days later, Jennifer White and Bob Lantinos were meeting at Bob's Washington office. She was finishing up her full report on the Mexico operation.

"But there's no doubt," Jennie said, "that these guys are part of a larger group – one of them thought that there were twenty men involved. He said that he had seen a burly guy meeting with the Chief and he knew that he was foreign because he had a strong accent which he thought he had heard in a movie with Yul Brynner. Probably Russian if what we know so far is true."

"Well, my gut is still with Ramsay," said Lantinos, "and probably Latchman, especially given what the other guy said."

After a few minutes of silence he went on. "Who the hell uses aboriginals? Only Ramsay could figure out a way. And so far, diamonds aren't bombs."

"You know Bob, in today's world there's no trouble getting guns, explosives, bombs...anything," said Jennifer. "Everything is available, including the people who know how to put it all together. The diamonds may be the distraction, but someone originally paid for them via Sierra Leone and is no doubt expecting to receive them."

"I think you're probably right. With another memo about P&M and Latchman in that bag holding the stones, you have to wonder what else is going on. What would diamonds have to do with Santino DeLuca's P&M fund," said Lantinos as he got up and stretched. "We had better meet with Larry Lyons soon. We need to bring him up to date and get his input on what our next step should be."

"Oh yeah, I forgot one thing," said Jennie. "That stupid 3rd hole reference. The guys said it was somewhere they had to be. They had no idea where it was."

CHAPTER SEVEN

Toronto, Ontario.

Two days later, Bob Lantinos arrived at Larry's office accompanied by Jennifer White, often referred to as the FBI's number one undercover agent. She was assigned to only the most difficult cases and though she had an incredible record of success, occasionally there were raised eyebrows about her "shoot first and ask questions later" attitude.

As Lantinos outlined the assignment and then offered the leadership role to him, Larry let out a whoop and jumped up from his chair to hug his friend.

Larry Lyons' past involvement in US and Canadian joint projects, along with his brother Grant Teasdale, who was almost a legend to some of the older law enforcement agents, reinforced the FBI's decision about Larry leading the way in this investigation. Larry was a happy-go-lucky type of guy with big brown eyes that he knew women loved and which he had no trouble using to get their attention. He was borderline skinny – he couldn't understand why all the steaks, ribs, lobster and roasted potatoes that he loved never showed up on his body, but he was happy about that. He was fifty-two years old and still couldn't find any gray in his dark blond hair. He got instant erections whenever he was in the right frame of mind – or body. He was an avid golfer with a 6 handicap, and he was a fan of Tiger Woods. He loved to argue with some of the female agents on his team about the merits of a great athlete's skill having nothing to do with their bizarre sexual preferences. He never won.

Larry was a former FBI agent who had joined the RCMP when he moved to Toronto years earlier to marry a local nurse. The marriage didn't last long, but his daughter Meghan was his "bonus" in life, and she was now a newly hired professor at McGill University in Montreal. He was determined to give her all the love and security he himself had never known.

Meghan was tall and slim with an elegant manner similar to her mother. She was bilingual and was now studying Mandarin in her spare time. Occasionally, Larry, who had a hard time expressing his personal feelings, would awkwardly ask about her personal life. This always evoked giggles from his daughter.

"Dad, you're such a hokey guy," she said with as much love as she could put into her voice. *"If you want to know something, just ask. For example, Meghan darling, are you dating anyone in particular? Meghan darling, are you in an intimate relationship with anyone?*

"Now I'm sure that your face is red Daddy dearest," she went on, still laughing. *"So you don't have to worry. If there is something I need to tell, you will be the first to know. I love you."*

Over the years he had risen in the ranks of law enforcement and was now at the "Inspector" level, though the designation was for the public record only. Larry Lyons was actually the head of INSETs, created by the prime minister after 9/11. Their mandate was to anticipate threats and pre-empt them on any level needed to protect Canada and its citizens. Drugs and money laundering were still the number one financiers of crime – crime that now included terrorism. INSETs existed to prevent, detect, deny and respond to criminal threats to Canada's national security. Given the joint border between the United States and Canada, this meant that both countries worked together as one when needed. During the next two hours of conversation, Larry was quite enthusiastic about the goals of the joint task force and the major players who were probably involved. Getting documented evidence would be a tough task. Snitches were not as easy to come by as they once were. Intelligence services had two basic ways of trying to catch the bad guys. They could use their superior technology to intercept communications either by the internet or "intergalactic stars" as Larry called it, or they could penetrate an organization with a turncoat or an undercover agent.

It was all contingent on what the parameters of the group were. The Russian mafia was more brutish than classy. The Chinese mafia definitely had superior brain skills, but their concern with face saving and appearances often bordered on egomania. The Italian mafia was still dependable – murder, retribution, *quid pro quo*. Larry liked them the best because he knew them.

Despite how exciting a challenge this project would be for Larry, he also had to face a harsh reality. It would have a personal hook that he knew would be tough for him to control – Elizabeth DeLuca. But control it he would.

No matter which way the world was going to turn, she would soon be in his life…again. He remembered the anguish he had once gone through because of her – and probably would again – and that was not a happy thought.

When he was a rookie agent, the FBI assigned him to follow Santino DeLuca on a flight to Boston. DeLuca wasn't on that plane, but his wife, Elizabeth, was. At the time, Larry had no idea who she was and no one in law enforcement knew how such a screw up had happened right under their noses.

When Larry finally took his seat after a fruitless search for Santino DeLuca and laid eyes on his blond seatmate, it was like a thunderbolt. He introduced himself as Larry Wilson. She smiled and told him that her name was Elizabeth Volpe. They chatted and when they found out they were staying at the same hotel they agreed to see some galleries and hockey games together. After two days, Larry knew that she was flirting with him. He made a move on her.

We had just come back to the hotel from a late supper and were still laughing when Elizabeth unlocked the door and I followed her into the room. I grabbed her and kissed her, gently at first, and then more intensely. She offered no resistance. In fact, when I felt her hand on my erection, I knew she was as aroused as I was. She responded to my kisses by running her tongue against my lips and moving her hands under my sweater towards my belt buckle.

Suddenly, she stopped and tried to push me away, but I was so aroused that I couldn't let her go.

"Larry, stop, stop, please! You have to stop! I'm married. I have children. Forgive me, please forgive me! You don't know who I am or anything about me. I had no right to lead you on this way. I pray that God will forgive me."

When Larry got back to Washington, he learned who she really was. As shocked as he was, it didn't change the way he felt about her, and over the years he followed the ongoing DeLuca saga via the investigations being run by his brother. Once in a while he found an excuse to call Elizabeth himself just to say hello and exchange pleasantries. She had no idea who he really was. Then DeLuca died. And a year later Larry, accompanied by his daughter Meghan, attended Santino DeLuca's memorial mass. Elizabeth's surprise could not hide the delight he saw in her eyes when she looked at him. But their passion for each other could not change the fact that, at the end of the day, he was a senior law enforcement officer moving up and she was the widow of an international crime boss. It couldn't work.

Now, sitting in his office looking out over Bay Street, Larry closed his eyes and relived his memories of her. He had enjoyed many women over the years, but there was only one Elizabeth. He loved her then and he loved her now. There would never be anyone else for him.

"Hey buddy, where are you?" asked Bob Lantinos jolting Larry back to the present. "You look like you are away in la la land. I hope my words aren't boring you."

Bob was still standing in front of his desk smiling at him. Jennifer was looking out the twenty-second floor window over Bay Street in the heart of Toronto's financial district.

"Nah, never!" answered Larry. "I was just having a memory moment."

CHAPTER EIGHT

Pte. St. Lucie, Florida.

Grant was running along the river listening to the sports report when the vibrator on his cellphone reminded him that business never took a holiday for him. He stopped and looked at the ID. It was his brother, Larry.

"Hello bro!" shouted Grant, as he continued running trying to keep listening out of one ear to the sports report on his iPod.

"Take off that stupid ear piece," laughed Larry. "How can you do two things at once?"

"I can do more than two things at once," yelled Grant into the mouthpiece. "Want details?"

"Spare me, please. This is business so I need your full attention."

Grant took off the iPod.

"Ok, done. What's going on?"

"I'll give you a brief outline now and more details when we meet," said Larry.

"Meet? Meet when?" asked Grant as he started moving his scheduled appointments and tasks around in his head.

"I need you to come up to Toronto," answered Larry. "It's pretty important, possibly even life altering. And some of the key figures are relevant to your past cases – and to the DeLucas."

Grant remained silent.

"Latchman and probably DeLuca – their current action. And a Canadian politician, Howard Ramsay. And Grant, P&M has something to do with it somehow. Listen, no telephone lines are safe as far as I'm concerned so only a walk in High Park will do as a good place to talk."

Still Grant didn't speak.

"I know you can hear me," said Larry. "And you know that I am making this call only after a lot of consideration on my part."

"Okay," Grant finally answered. "Sam is flying back home to Boston tomorrow and I always go with him. I'll get a connecting flight to Toronto from there."

"It's nice to know I can always count on you," said Larry with a warm smile on his face. "Give Lisa and Sam a hug for me. Let me know specific times and I'll have someone pick you up at the airport. You'll stay with me. Maybe a couple of days are all we need."

Grant smiled as he thought about his brother and the first time he'd seen him – in that hellhole of an orphanage so many years ago.

Larry had been crying for so long that I got up and went over to sit down on his cot. The little boy threw his arms around my neck and held on so tightly that I felt myself transported back in time to when my parents and baby brother Kevin had been alive. I cuddled the trembling child and rocked him back and forth, remembering how warm and comfortable it used to feel being held by someone who loved me.

After Larry fell asleep, I got down on my knees beside his cot and prayed, something I hadn't done since my own family had died.

Somehow I'll take care of you and maybe make a life for us when I grow up. Please God, help me.

Grant took a couple of deep breaths and turned to stare out across the river. He knew that Larry would not have called if it wasn't crucial to his investigation. He always knew that there would be unfinished business relevant to the DeLucas and that Rebecca would've had a hand in it.

He closed his eyes and once again he was back in time. But this time he was in a Niagara Falls motel room meeting with Johnny Brattini.

"Rebecca was a special woman who managed to get under my skin," Brattini said. "I'm quite anxious to know the why and who relevant to her death. I will be looking into matters from here. However, I'm afraid that I won't be able to share anything that I find out with you."

I smiled at him. "I didn't expect you to, but Rebecca believed that she had some information that might be of help and asked me to deliver it to you personally."

Brattini turned white. "What do you mean by that?"

"She wrote me a letter just before her death," I answered, amused at Brattini's fear of the supernatural. "She expected repercussions from her confrontations and wanted to put her affairs in order before it was too late."

We talked well into the night, finishing a bottle of brandy between us, and before he left, I gave Brattini a copy of an infamous video recording...along with some other material.

"If you need me, I'll be in my Florida office," I said as I got up to leave. "Rebecca believed that you had no responsibility in her death, and that if you had been able to, you would have stopped it."

"Yes, I would have," answered Johnny emphatically. "And I will find out everything that I need to know. You understand that it must be dealt with in my own way, which is not necessarily yours."

"Yes, I understand," I said with a sigh as I shook Brattini's hand. "As long as it gets done."

Even though it was so many years ago, some things never ran out of time until all the scores were settled. Only he and Brattini held the damaging evidence against Ramsay that Rebecca once had. And deep down Grant knew Rebecca and that evidence had something to do with Ramsay, Latchman and this investigation, and so the time for the settlements had arrived. Years ago, Grant had told Brattini that he didn't need to know the details Brattini might gather. But now he needed to find out everything, and he needed Brattini to help. If Ramsay was looking to settle old scores, Grant knew that Sam and Lisa might be at risk.

He headed off towards his car. He had to call Lisa and then arrange to get his appointments rescheduled. And prepare for what he knew was coming.

CHAPTER NINE

Boston, Massachusetts.

Giancarlo (Johnny) Brattini, boss of the Salerno crime family, stood well over six feet tall with black hair and steely gray eyes. His home, which sat on three-and-a-half acres of landscaped gardens overlooking Lake Erie just outside of Buffalo, New York, had a state-of-the-art gym where he worked out four times a week with his personal trainer. He was rich and powerful, and according to the media that loved writing about him, must be a very happy man. But instead, he was driven, ruthless and lonely, with no recollection of ever having received any affection or respect from his father, no matter how hard he had tried to please him. The best he ever got was a pat on the head or an occasional grunt of approval. Johnny didn't have the sensitivity to understand that his father's lifetime, one filled with violence and hurt, had long buried Massimo Brattini's ability to show physical affection.

Over the years, Johnny's father had taken him around the country introducing him to people and circumstances that were a part of the world in which they both lived. By the time he was eighteen, Johnny had earned the respect, and the fear, of many men on both sides of the law. But before he joined the "business" full time, Massimo insisted that his son go to college. It was his expression of love for his son, which Johnny never figured out.

"Let him have a carefree and happy time to remember when he is older," Massimo had said to his wife Donna. "Not like me."

During the years that Johnny attended college, he never let down his guard. He didn't know how. He played basketball well enough to be on the B team, but he rarely socialized with any of the guys beyond a drink at the local pub. The co-eds were always ready for him. He was a powerful lover who knew how to use his tongue and fingers to make them happy. But to him, it was just a means to his own end – sexual gratification and dominance.

When he met Marsha Palozzo she was quiet and easily intimated despite being the niece of Vincent Palozzo, boss of the Cleveland crime family. They had gravitated to each other at first more out of empathy than passion, given the notoriety of both their families. But she had a wonderful smile, a gorgeous body, and she looked at him with such adoration that he decided that she was going to be his wife. After they got married their life together had been steady and uneventful; their three daughters' lives, much the same. Johnny was as happy as he thought that he could ever be and had never cheated on Marsha, a rare virtue in his circle of friends and associates.

As the years passed and his power within the family grew, Johnny became more and more like his late father, even down to the rimless glasses he wore. His language skills were more polished and his demeanour more elegant, but underneath the surface he was still Massimo Brattini's son…and a killer.

His late father and Santino DeLuca had been bitter enemies. Johnny had spent his upbringing learning about and living within their families' rivalry. But now that his sister Angela was happily married to Peter DeLuca, both families had evolved into a hostile truce – more to avoid the eyes of the law but also due to a softening of their mutual hatred.

It was March and a snowstorm had closed the Buffalo airport, so Johnny was stuck in Boston for another day. He decided to call Lisa Sherman and invite her out for lunch. No pressure, no business, no politics.

For so many years, Rebecca Sherman's involvement with DeLuca made her an enemy as well. But after Massimo and Santino were both gone, Rebecca and Johnny came to greatly respect each other. He told himself that it was out of respect for her memory that he kept tabs on Lisa, but he knew that wasn't the reason. Despite his best efforts, Johnny was growing more and more attracted to her.

To Johnny's delight, Lisa quickly accepted his invitation.

Johnny had kept in touch with Lisa as the years passed, but he had never made a serious move on her even though he wanted to. He enjoyed their fun flirtations and teasing banter and he accepted that as all there was…for the time being. Their friendship had strengthened even as her life took some strange turns. He continued to try to push his sexual desire for her along with his lewd thoughts away – though with the passage of time that was becoming more difficult – even as their world continued to turn.

When Lisa came out of her front door with a big smile, he was stunned, as he always was, at how attractive she was. His driver opened the door and they hugged once she was inside the car.

"What a good idea this was," she said. "Sam is still in Florida and Isobel and I are having some issues."

"Oh," said Johnny, not really wanting to hear about it. "I hope everything will be okay." The relationship that Lisa had with Isobel was something he wiped from his brain. He didn't care what it meant; as a man, he knew that she was a woman, and a very sensuous woman. So whatever fixation she was in right now, there was nothing about it that he was going to think about.

"But since I'm stuck in Boston for another day," he went on before she could answer, "I thought we could have a fun lunchtime *kibitz*. I haven't had a chance to touch base with you in a while."

"How are Marsha and the girls?" asked Lisa as the car took off. "Angela told me that she is joining them on a spa trip to Florida next week. I'm jealous."

They soon arrived at the Lobster Hut restaurant. Once they were settled and each had a glass of wine, Johnny was delighted to see how Lisa was flirting with him. She kept her big brown eyes glued to his while he spoke, and then, when the moment was right, slowly lowered them.

This is insane, he thought, feeling like he was eighteen years old.

"Well, I can see by the way you are looking at me that you are thinking of making a move," whispered Lisa with a bright smile. "Have you ever cheated on Marsha?"

Before he could answer she went on, "And you are kind of cute. But I understand that you aren't Jewish."

Johnny burst out laughing, knowing that she was playing with him and trying to get him flustered. *Oh, how I want you,* he thought. *And I am going to have to tell you about the past if I ever want to have a future with you.*

After they had finished their lobsters and were contemplating dessert, Johnny said, "Lisa, there is actually some stuff that I want to tell you about."

"You look serious," said Lisa as she finished her wine.

"I am," he answered with a smile. "But you have known me long enough to know that I'm not a very good public speaker. So be patient with me and I'll talk as fast as I can and then you can ask me any questions you want."

"Okay," she said, flashing her dimples and smile. "Shoot."

Oh my god! What a word choice, he thought, as images of Lisa's mother Rebecca flashed in front of him.

"Once upon a time," he began, ignoring Lisa's burst of laughter at his opening line, "Massimo Brattini and Santino DeLuca were enemies, and in our world, that meant no holds barred. Your mother's involvement with DeLuca made her my enemy as well."

The smile left Lisa's face and she kept her eyes glued to his.

"Many years ago your mother and I had an altercation in an old railway depot," he continued. "We both had guns and we both fired them. She missed and I didn't."

"Is that when you picked me up at the airport?" she asked.

"Yes," he answered quietly. "Luckily, and happily, my aim was almost as bad as hers and she recovered. Even though it happened so long ago, I wanted to tell you about it, in confidence, so that there would be a genuine open and honest relationship between us.

"And I was also lucky that your mother missed my head, or we wouldn't be here today enjoying each other's company." He tried to half smile. Lisa's eyes filled as she took a deep breath.

"And to answer your unasked question," Johnny went on, "I had nothing to do with that car bomb."

Finally she said, "Elizabeth has always told me that the ties between the Brattinis and the DeLucas were complicated. And that nothing between all of you was black or white. She also wanted me to know that I could trust you and that Sam could always count on you. That has meant a lot to me, given your line of work."

Despite himself, Johnny burst out laughing again. *Oh God, you are so fabulous!*

"Okay," said Johnny as he waved for the bill. "You know what you need to know. I wanted to make sure that there were no dark secrets left between us. And now life can move on."

Once they were standing by the entrance waiting for Johnny's car. Lisa turned and wrapped her arms around him, putting her cheek against his.

"In another time and place, maybe even in another world, who knows?" she whispered in his ear. "But not in this one."

We'll see. We'll see, Johnny thought.

CHAPTER TEN

Toronto, Ontario.

As long as Teasdale had no objections, Jennie would be staying on to work this project. Looking at Jennie, it would be hard for anyone, especially a man, to have objections to her presence. Almost six feet tall, she had ash blond hair and sparkling green eyes with a body to die for. Jennie had wanted to be an FBI agent ever since she had been a teenager. Her parents had been horrified when they learned that she really intended to be a "G-woman." When she graduated from Mount Holyoke College in 1995 she knew that her first choice for a career had not changed despite her parents' entreaties that she "think it over just a little bit longer."

Jennie applied to the FBI the day after her twenty-third birthday. Given her superb education that included majors in accounting and math, along with her excellent physical condition, she had been accepted right away and sent off to Quantico for fifteen months of additional training. She was devoted to her career in law enforcement – was sometimes ruthless and had tunnel vision when it came to solving a crime or tracking undercover drugs and terrorists – and was working at becoming the first female Director of the FBI. She had no doubts about her abilities and lots of confidence in her own judgement.

By choice she had never married and had only taken lovers of her choosing with no commitments ever made. Jennie's parents had been loving and attentive and there were no underlying traumas or rejections in her life that would have driven her to seek satisfaction in affairs. She had no desire to experience motherhood; she was content to play at it with her sister Jane's children.

She loved sex and would try anything once. She often wondered why she was almost as interested in sexual dalliances as she was in catching the bad guys. The truth was really quite simple: she loved men and really liked working on the body, no pun intended, of a man she wanted. Most of her lovers were in the law enforcement field, but occasionally she went after others, but never anyone involved in the investigations she was working or anyone in the fitness or health field.

The first group was obvious – too many problems and complications when one mixed business and pleasure – she never did. The second group loved themselves and their bodies too much – they had no time to think about their partner. Besides, they were boring with nothing of interest to talk about except themselves.

The reality of her life was that there were very few people with whom she could share the details of what her job really involved and even fewer who would tolerate her frequent and often unplanned absences. Leaving at a moment's notice to go off to deal with dangerous and often unspeakable things wasn't exactly the way to build a happy home life. Missed anniversaries, birthday parties, soccer games, school plays – family and a stable home life only worked when a resilient and unique spouse was prepared to put up with it in order to keep the family strong and together. But the best of intentions, backed up by the stats on the divorce rate among law enforcement officers, rarely worked. Jennie didn't bother trying.

As Jennie and Lantinos headed out onto Bay Street from Larry Lyons' office, the sun was just breaking through a very cloudy morning. Of course, Bay Street was like New York – tall buildings on either side of the street with just a glimmer of light in between.

"Are you going back to Washington right away?" asked Jennie.

"Yes, as soon as I can get to the airport. I've got too much stuff still waiting for me."

"Why the rush?" she asked. "Nothing much can happen until Latchman gets back from Kiev."

"I know, I know," answered Lantinos. "But I've been around these guys for years and just when you think you have it figured out, something falls out of the blue. And I'm worried about Ramsay. He has tentacles everywhere, especially in the Canadian government. And if the rumours about the aboriginals turn out to be more than that, he will warn them before he covers his ass with someone else. And now that we know about his ties to Latchman, time is even trickier for us."

"Okay, but let's walk around the block," said Jennie. "I want to know more about Grant Teasdale before I meet him, and I also want to know about his relationship with his brother. Why don't they have the same last name? And Teasdale's involvement with Rebecca Sherman is interesting, to say the least. Apparently, she was the brains behind some of DeLuca's money machinations years ago. No conflicts for Teasdale?"

"Well," sighed Lantinos. "Leave those questions for now. The story of Larry Lyons and Grant Teasdale is as compelling as anything you will ever hear.

"Teasdale's parents had immigrated to Canada from Ireland in the late fifties. They were living in a small town in northern Ontario with two sons – Grant and a new baby – when a fire destroyed their small frame house. Luckily Grant had been in school when it happened and since there were no relatives in Canada, the local priest arranged for him to be placed in the Brothers of St. John Orphanage.

"When Larry Lyons arrived there two years later, he was only five years old. His mother was a local prostitute who had abandoned him at the front gates.

"There were forty boys in the orphanage, the oldest was sixteen. Beatings were administered regularly to all the boys, no matter what their age or what the infraction. Grant took over as Larry's guardian and older brother in order to protect him. Sexual abuse was rampant in that orphanage and three of the trustees, who were men over forty-five years of age, were eventually tried, convicted and jailed as pedophiles.

"RCMP Inspector Brian Teasdale was the lead investigator and was so moved by the plight of the two boys that he brought them home to meet his wife, Janet. They had no children of their own and they adopted the two boys.

"The new family thrived together; the boys grew into successful men, both in the law enforcement field.

"Grant had taken the Teasdale name right after the adoption, but Larry never did. When I once asked him about it he said that he was hoping that one day his mother would come back to find him. So that is a tough one."

Jennie turned her head away from him, but not before he saw the tears in her eyes.

"There is a special strength in both of them," Lantinos continued, "that many of us never have to find in ourselves – and a ruthless determination. Luckily, they both work for us. But never forget where they've been and what they've endured."

CHAPTER ELEVEN

Boston, Massachusetts.

"Hi Lisa," said Grant when she picked up the telephone. "Everything ok with you?"

"Not really," she answered. "Isobel and I seem to be coming to the end of the road. I hoped that these two weeks with Sam at your place would help us rekindle some of the old feelings. But it's not to be. Ugh! I hate the stress and uncertainty that's about to drop on me."

"I told you a long time ago that I thought Isobel was a temporary respite in your life," said Grant as gently as he could. "The two of you got into a comfort zone that has run out of time. In fact, it ran out of time five years ago. And if you hadn't been so busy in your separate worlds it would have ended even before that."

"Of course, you are probably right," answered Lisa. "The good news is that I don't think Sam will care one way or another. They got along, of course, but she wasn't into brilliant boys (Grant smiled) and Sam wasn't impressed with her medical degree.

"Anyhow, why are we talking about this on the telephone? We can do a sit down when you get here tomorrow."

"Actually, that's why I'm calling you now," answered Grant. "I won't have time to do that. I need you to call Elizabeth and ask her to go to a payphone and call me at home in about an hour. Remind to her to bring enough change."

"Why do I have a sinking feeling in my stomach?" mumbled Lisa as her heart froze. "Something has obviously happened."

"No, nothing has happened…yet," he said. "But I need to speak to Elizabeth first. I'll fill you in, as much as I can, at the airport tomorrow. Lucky Sam will get to play the video games he always bugs me about while you and I talk. I won't have much time. I am going up to Toronto directly from there."

"Grant, should I be scared?" asked Lisa. "Is this the time we have always known would come? Is Sam is any danger?"

"Neither one of you will ever be in any danger," he answered forcefully. "I am always right here with you. You should know that by now. But some loose ends have to be sewn up once and for all, and I'm not yet sure who is going to be the sewer and who is going to be the loose end."

Lisa took a couple of deep breaths before she continued to speak with more confidence than she was feeling.

"I trust you, completely Grant," she said. "I always will. You've never let us down. I'll see you tomorrow."

Elizabeth sat in the phone booth almost in a trance for ten minutes after she and Grant had finished their conversation. All those platitudes used by so many people for so many reasons for so many years now hit her in the gut – "full circle," "what goes around comes around," "final nail in the coffin." Her family was at risk, again – a family that now included Lisa Sherman and her son, Sam – Sam, who she loved as she loved Peter's two daughters. They were all hers and they were only alive because of Rebecca Sherman – and that was a reality that Elizabeth accepted. Rebecca had helped Elizabeth when Bob DeSalle once again tried to kill her. He failed when she was fourteen, and if it weren't for Rebecca he might have succeeded on his second try so many years later. If it's true what Grant said, and Ramsay and Latchman are together again, they are no doubt trying to finish the job that DeSalle couldn't. Elizabeth knew she had to help Grant Teasdale and Larry Lyons; she had to keep her family safe.

Larry Lyons. Thinking of him gave her heart a jolt...as usual. She would have to see him again – work with him, cooperate with him and trust in his judgement, and Grant's, to save them all.

It had been so many years since Larry Lyons first came into her life. Years later, after Santino's death, Larry had shown up at Santino's memorial mass with his daughter, Meghan. Elizabeth remembered how her heart had started pounding when she looked up and saw him standing in front of her. And then some weeks later...in a flash she was back in time.

"Larry, what are you doing here?" I gasped when I opened the door. "How did you know that I was here in Toronto?"

He said nothing as he took me in his arms and kissed me. I immediately responded by wrapping my arms around his neck and pressing my body against his.

"Elizabeth, Elizabeth," Larry whispered in my ear. "You've been in my head for so long."

The towel that I had wrapped around my body slipped to the floor. His hands moved up the sides of my legs and around my buttocks. His caresses were gentle on my skin and when his hands reached my breasts, my nipples were already hard in anticipation of his touch. He lowered his head and began to lick them as my body pulsed with ecstasy.

My hands ran through his hair and my lips moved along his shoulders as he continued sucking and nibbling on my breasts. His hand slid up between my legs and even before he slipped his fingers inside me, he knew how wet he would find me.

My hands moved around Larry's waist and unclipped his belt and then the buttons on his pants. I slipped my hands inside and he groaned in response to my stroking his penis. We stood locked together, our hands and fingers stimulating each other to the point of explosion.

Suddenly Larry pulled me down onto the floor and spread my legs, leaning over my face, kissing my eyes, my lips, my neck, and then back up again to my lips.

"I want you so much," he whispered, gazing into my eyes as his fingers stroked my clitoris and my body writhed underneath his hand. "You're so wet!"

"Now!" I cried out to him. "I want you inside of me now!"

He tore off his pants and pushed himself deep into me, his hands grasping my buttocks as he pulled me closer. I wrapped my legs around his back and pulled his mouth down to mine until he gave himself up to the tremors that pulsed through his body.

"Yes! Yes!" I cried against his lips. "Don't stop what you are doing to me, please don't ever stop!"

CHAPTER TWELVE

Toronto, Ontario.

Grant and Larry were having a drink and catching up on family news while they waited for Jennifer White to join them for dinner.

Grant had flown in from Boston two hours earlier, having left Sam with his mother and Nonna Elizabeth at the airport. Lisa tried very hard to be casual and unconcerned about the events that appeared to be shaking both Elizabeth and Grant during their brief conversation. When Sam, barely able to contain his glee, had been let loose at the game machines, the three of them had a quick conversation. Grant had seen through Lisa's attempts at bravado and kept his arm around her shoulder.

"Lisa, I have nothing more to tell you," I said. "When I get to Toronto I have a meeting with Larry and the FBI agent working with him. All I know is that some information was uncovered during a couple of undercover operations that causes me concern, and that concern is prompting me to take an in-depth look at some old investigations, including the DeLuca investigation.

"I insisted the FBI provide some extra security for you as well as Elizabeth if I was going to help them. And don't make that face, Lisa. Hopefully it won't be needed beyond a few weeks or until we get this matter resolved. There will be someone on Sam and a watch on your house. These are the specialists of Homeland Security and they won't be noticed by Sam. Help me make it move as fast as possible by not *creating a buzz. Just be a little more vigilant and let me know if anything seems out of place or unusual or even if either of you just get a feeling that something isn't right."*

"So I spoke to Kevin yesterday," said Larry as the waiter brought him a vodka on ice. "I got a birthday card in the mail with some drawings and a happy face, so I called him. Did you know that?"

Grant's face lit up. "No, I didn't know, but that is so fantastic," he answered. "The Home tries to maintain regular, family involvements so the kids, and I guess lots of them are not really kids anymore, feel part of a normal family dynamic. He also sends cards to Lisa and Sam for their birthdays and for special holidays. But Kevin is pretty advanced, at least advanced in terms of developmental disabilities. A ten year old knows how to do lots of things and can figure out lots of things. Unfortunately, he is in a man's body."

"Well, the Christopher Robin Home is the best," said Larry. "There was no hesitation on getting Kevin to the phone – I'm sure someone was there with him – but he was so excited to hear from me and I felt so good about it.

"And I was really surprised that his last words to me were about how he would see me at Sam's bar mitzvah. It was absolute clarity. It was really something."

"Too bad Brian and Janet didn't live to see how far Kevin has come along," said Grant quietly. "What incredible people they were. They had love for all of us. I can only hope that they are now in the special place that Janet certainly believed existed."

Grant sensed the stirring of people around him before Larry stood up with a wide grin on his face.

"Hi Jennie, glad you found your way."

Grant stood up and turned around. *Wham! Bam!* That's what was spinning in his head as he looked at a woman whom he could only describe as breathtaking. Jennie was wearing slim black silk slacks, a V-necked gray silk blouse that clung to her breasts, leaving a tantalizing cleavage that Grant was definitely noticing, and a black leather jacket draped over her arm.

"Hello there gentlemen," said Jennie as she met Grant's stare without blinking.

"Hey, I'm over here," laughed Larry as he watched the two of them start the dance of seduction.

Grant moved first. He took her hand, smiled and said, "Your reputation as a first-class agent precedes you. But nothing could have prepared me for how beautiful you are."

Ah shit, what a hokey line.

"Ah, Inspector Teasdale," Jennie practically moaned in response. "Thank you for your kind words. Despite being a cop, I still love to hear sweet words from a handsome man."

Oh god! What a stupid answer.

The two of them were staring at each other, hands still joined, when Larry poked them both.

"Okay people, time for dinner and business. You can make your appointment for later."

All three of them laughed and sat down. And business took over.

"I heard about the Mexican takedown," Grant said after the main course was cleared from the table. "How the hell did you manage to get out of that one?"

"Not easily," answered Jennie. "Especially when two of the runners were aboriginals trying to pass themselves off as part of the Sinaloa cartel. However, nothing will give you away faster than trying to speak Spanish with an aboriginal accent.

"Of course, I got lucky," she continued. "Just before Mexico there was a small event at the border crossing in Cornwall. We were following what was supposed to be a large cash transfer of several million dollars. When the deal blew up, literally, the millions in cash turned out to be a large cache of raw diamonds hidden in a very heavy sack of coloured stones. One of the couriers babbled for about a minute into my wire before he died.

"When the wiretap was being analyzed," she went on, "I was there listening to the CSI do his review. The dead guy's accent was distinctive. So it looks like at least one of the aboriginals killed in Cornwall and three of those killed in Juárez spoke the same dialect.

And that reinforces the concern that a distinctive group of runners, probably no more than ten, is being trained on a specific assignment."

"We think this is a different kind of scheme," Larry added for Grant's benefit. "Washington is concerned about Howard Ramsay and his access to US top secret communications with the new prime minister. Jake Bartoli is actually more than concerned. He thinks that Ramsay has his hand in money transfers for a Russian mobster – Yuri Latchman – transfers from Israel."

"So what?" snapped Grant, a deep pain already filling his gut just hearing the words "Howard Ramsay." *The envelope Rebecca left me. The evidence that I gave Brattini.*

"So what?" answered Larry. "I'll tell you so what. If Ramsay has established a pack of runners and they are aboriginals, that means more than money and drugs can be moved across the border."

"Explosives, bombs?" asked Grant, still incredulous. "Why?"

"Why?" answered Larry.

"What are you, a broken record?" laughed Jennie.

"Again, why?" said Larry. "Because Latchman has a diamond smuggling operation in Kiev. It's funding the Russian president's off-the-record private ventures as well as paying off some of his old debts. Latchman needs Ramsay to keep the doors open so he can provide his Russian friends with untraceable fireworks. Right now, with all the anti-American flare-ups in the Middle East, very little attention is being paid to Russia and its own issues. Bombings and suicide attacks elsewhere distract their people. And that is the way they want it."

"But why would Ramsay be involved in this?" asked Grant, already knowing the answer.

"I think he is just an egomaniac," answered Jennie. "And if he can make sure that he's the man to see to get goods, even highly dangerous goods, moved across the border, then that will be priceless for him. He knows that he'll have to arrange to get whatever it is into Canada first so he can then easily get it into the United States. His access to all those faceless civil servants who sign waivers, who sign approvals, who hate the Conservatives, who love the Muslims – look how many of them and their families own property in Québec and Ontario. And now we're hearing about British Columbia as well. This will put incredible power into Ramsay's hands."

"So now we have to get evidence," Larry said emphatically. "We haven't been able to do it all these years, but now, after the two takedowns we talked about, we might have a chance. So we must find out who else is working with them, especially if it is someone in the government.

"Luckily for us, the guys used on both these runs were pretty useless," he went on, "and they sang like canaries in Juárez, thanks to Jennie."

"Okay," said Grant. "Give me a synopsis of what you have and then we can make a plan."

"Well, I have a bad feeling about all this," said Grant after Jennie had finished bringing them up to date on Mexico. As he drank his cappuccino, Jennifer was having fun with a big bowl of ice cream. When Larry and Grant started talking, she knew it was time to just keep her mouth shut and listen.

"Rebecca herself wasn't sure about Latchman when she met him," Grant confessed to Larry. "She warned me to keep an eye on him. Larry, in the note Rebecca wrote me before she died, she guessed Latchman would have a role in her imminent murder.

"And as far as Ramsay is concerned, Rebecca was the reason he never got a chance to run for public office. She had damaging information on him and he knew it. That twit thought he was prime ministerial material, but he didn't dare pursue it. I think this whole DeLuca – Brattini exercise has come full circle. Latchman is associated with Peter DeLuca – not in everything, but certainly in enough deals to raise a red herring. Brattini knows a different side of the Latchman clan, whether he's involved or not. And Ramsay and Latchman have too many ties with Rebecca to ignore. The fact that they're working together is more than suspicious."

"Well, what is the next move on your part?" asked Larry.

"There's only one way to go," answered Grant. "We have to put all of them – the DeLucas, the Brattinis and my Rebecca's daughter in one room. It is time to put all the details together, and there can be no conditions or restrictions. With evidence somehow linking P&M with Latchman and Ramsay, Rebecca's past has something to do with their new business relationship. I can't take a chance if Lisa and Sam are at risk.

"And Larry, you'll have to be there as well," he went on. "I know that Brattini and DeLuca have information on Latchman and Ramsay that can help us. We are missing something when it comes to this investigation. It will be your credibility and commitment that offers the only chance for Peter, and especially Johnny Brattini, to agree to cooperate."

Then Grant smiled and said, "Of course, all this can only happen with Elizabeth's help. Only she can bring everyone around the table. I've told her my concerns, and she's already agreed to help."

"Hey, guys, even though you are ignoring me, I'm still here," smiled Jennifer.

"How could I ever forget that?" Grant said with a smile. "Would you like to take a walk with me after we leave and then I'll drive you home?"

"Okay, sounds great," smiled Jennifer. *He won't have to ask twice.*

"Larry, I'm sure you can find your way home without me."

"Sure," smiled Larry. "I've got a good book to read."

"Mmm," purred Jennifer as Grant massaged her neck. "You are the most delicious man."

"And you, Madam," he said as his hands slipped around her shoulders and over to her breasts, "could turn on a zombie."

"Stay here with me tonight," she whispered turning onto her back and spreading her legs. "Larry won't miss you – and besides, this is business."

"Yah, some business," murmured Grant as he kissed her and slipped his fingers inside her at the same time. "With you around, I'm sure I'll never retire."

CHAPTER THIRTEEN

Boston, Massachusetts.

The group milling around in the den of the DeLuca townhouse was silent.

Angela and Peter DeLuca were sitting together on the couch. He had his arm around her shoulder. Angela Brattini DeLuca was a stunning young woman with jet black hair and a wonderful smile. Though officially the daughter of the late Donna and Massimo Brattini, she was actually the biological daughter of Bob DeSalle – a fact only disclosed by Donna Brattini shortly before her death twelve years earlier.

Johnny Brattini was standing off by himself next to the patio door. Johnny had some difficulty adjusting when he learned that his "sweet baby Angela" was only his half-sister; the thought of how his father had been cuckolded bothered him for a long time. But that time had passed and Johnny and Angela were now as close as they had once been. "Half is as good as whole," he often said when they were together and he was teasing her about something or other.

Matthew DeLuca, fraternal twin brother of Peter DeLuca, was sitting on one of the bar stools nibbling on a bowl of cashews. He had been assigned to the Vatican since his ordination ten years earlier. He had the most wonderful smile and was adored by all his nieces and his special nephew, Sam Teasdale. Lisa Sherman was sitting next to Matthew at the bar.

Grant Teasdale was standing in front of the bookcase wall next to his brother, Larry.

All of the people in the room had ties to each other – some had been bound a generation earlier. Peter DeLuca and Johnny Brattini were not the vicious enemies that their late fathers had once been, but the two of them were still competitors in the gray area of their financial operations.

When Elizabeth DeLuca, widow of Santino and mother of Peter and Matthew, came into the room, she was the epitome of elegance. Her ash blond hair was now short and her green eyes still shone like emeralds. Even in this circumstance, she was wearing Donna Karan. She was carrying two bottles of Merlot and a large bowl of crackers, cheese and shrimp. She put everything down on the sideboard and took out wine glasses, bottled water and plates. No one moved.

Grant took charge. "Okay, everyone, get something to eat before Elizabeth has a fit. Then I need you all to sit down and listen very carefully."

It didn't take ten minutes for everyone to get some food and a glass of wine.

"It looks like we're ready," Grant continued. "Please don't interrupt until I'm done. Then you can say anything you want.

"Two people who are not here but are aware of this meeting and what we are going to work out are Jennifer White, an undercover FBI agent, and her boss, Robert Lantinos. As you know, or maybe you all don't know, Larry Lyons is here as the head of INSETs. He has the authorization of both the Canadian government and the FBI to act in any way he sees fit." Heads turned to nod at Larry.

"Information came to Larry's attention, which he then passed on to me. It concerned a smuggling operation in Cornwall, Ontario, and later a drug bust in Mexico. Regardless of whether some of you know about this already," Grant said as he glanced first at Peter and then at Johnny, "we know that the key players in this operation have ties to both your families, and so we're here to ask for your help.

"I have reason to believe that the lives of my son Sam and his mother Lisa are at risk. No matter what I have to do or who I have to neutralize, I will not allow anything to happen to them. Some of us know a few of the reasons, but for the first time in fifty years, we are all going to know everything. I expect any of you with relevant information to share it – because we will eventually find out anyhow – and then we can work together to fix the problem, permanently.

"To that end I have called in all my chips; some are over thirty years old," he went on. "That's why Larry is here – and why all of you will be immune from any repercussions from this case in terms of the information you share with me today. As well, you will be immune from anything you might have been involved in years ago relevant only to this matter and for any events that might necessarily occur in the future."

There was silence.

"Ok," said Grant. "In order to understand how and why we are in this situation, we have to start at the beginning. Elizabeth, your words are the key…along with the audio tape you have brought for us to hear."

"I am going to share with all of you as many details as I can remember," said Elizabeth to no one in particular. "I'm telling you this because I'm convinced that Grant's concern is real. His investigation is going to involve my family. We all remember power broker Bob DeSalle – Rebecca's political colleague and Santino's friend. And we all remember his disappearance. Now you'll find out who he really was and what happened to him, because this all starts with DeSalle. It was such a long time ago. I'll do my best to be as specific as I can.

"Before Santino died, he asked me to bring Rebecca Sherman to see him. For obvious reasons I was reluctant, but I knew he would never ask this of me if it wasn't important."

"Hello Rebecca," I blurted out quickly when she answered her phone. "I know you must be surprised to hear from me after so many years, but Santino has asked me to call you. He is very ill and wants to see you."

It was four o'clock in the morning when she arrived the next day.

"Thank you for coming Rebecca," I said. "It means a lot to all of us. Santino is fairly sedated most of the time. But he wanted to make sure that he was awake and alert when he saw you, so we have cut down on his painkillers."

As we walked silently towards the elevator that would take us up to Santino's room, I stopped and took her arm.

"Massimo Brattini arrived here weeks ago to pay his last respects to Santino, and I noticed how he kept looking at me strangely. When Peter and Matthew had come into the den to talk to him I became even more uneasy by the intensity of his stares. He had hovered around the boys, questioning them about their activities and constantly putting his arm on their shoulders. When I took him up to see Santino, I had already hidden one of my sons' tape recorders under the skirted table next to the bed. I clicked it on when I left the room. Massimo never noticed it.

"So when you talk to Santino, know that I am aware of everything he is going to tell you, or almost everything. And because of what I have done, I'm ready to do anything necessary to help."

At first, Rebecca was silent. Then she said, "I would like to listen to the conversation between Brattini and Santino before I go up to see Santino."

"I thought you would. I have it right here."

Elizabeth stood up from her chair and pressed play on an old portable tape recorder that was resting on the table in front of her. Everyone leaned in to listen; the age of the recorder made the sound fuzzy. The first voice heard was that of Santino DeLuca.

"Hello Massimo, it's been a long time," he said. Everyone was quiet as they listened to the two men exchanged pleasantries, the usual gossip about former friends and enemies and the latest predictions on the soccer matches, especially whether or not Italy would ever regain its world title. Then Brattini began his narrative on why he had come to visit.

"Bob DeSalle is coming here to kill your wife and children, and if he has time, you as well, at least that's what he says."

Angela Brattini DeLuca sat up and squeezed Peter's hand. "Oh my God," she whispered and put her head on her husband's shoulder. "This is unreal."

"Are you nuts?" Santino's voice choked. "Why the fuck would he want to do that?"

"Because you don't really know the full story about Elizabeth's birth," said Massimo. "I am here to tell it to you.

"A long time ago there were two girls walking along a country road in Puglia – Giovanna Volpe and Theresa Vincenzo. Three drunken soldiers grabbed them and dragged them into the woods next to a small lake. When things got really ugly one of the soldiers tried to intervene and was knocked out by the other two. When he woke up his friends had just stripped Giovanna and were about to work on her. Theresa's dead body was lying next to her. He persuaded them to let him go first. They agreed and walked away. Then he used every technique he had ever read or heard about to try and make it easier for her. And when it was done, he told her to pretend she was suffering and scream loudly so he could throw her in the water with her hands loosely tied as though she were unconscious. It worked and Giovanna Volpe lived. She gave birth to a daughter nine months later...and named her Elizabeth.

"The dead girl, Theresa Vincenzo, was the sister of Roberto Vincenzo, who changed his name to Bob DeSalle when he came to the United States. Her grandfather, Don Paolo, eventually tracked down the rapists, the Luchese brothers, who he believed had acted alone. His men butchered both of them.

"And the third guy? The one who had raped Giovanna as gently as he could and who she protected and who was the biological father of Elizabeth? The guy who escaped to the United States and wound up leading the Salerno family? His name? Massimo Brattini!"

"Oh my God!" Santino's voice moaned. "Oh no!"

Matthew got off the bar stool and walked over to his mother. "Are you okay?" he asked her in a very gentle voice as he took her hand.

She nodded silently.

"Yes Santino, it is true," continued Massimo after a pause. "During all these years I have never forgotten Giovanna – I didn't even know her name back then. When I escaped to the United States three weeks after the attack, I didn't know how to find her. I never even knew she had been knocked up. When I found out I went back to Italy and tracked her down. When I saw her again I realized that I had loved her from that first moment fifty years earlier. We only had a few days together; it was like a dream. Then, two weeks after that, she died.

"Your wife is my daughter and your sons are my grandsons."

For a few minutes they heard only the sound of static from the tape. Then Brattini broke the silence.

"Vincenzo came to my office and told me that he had learned that Elizabeth was not killed in that explosion he had set up in Rome years ago – you had saved her. He told me how he wanted to pull the trigger himself. He was raving about how he let his grandfather down, how his sister's death has gone unavenged all these years because one of the rapist's children still lived. And if not for you saving Elizabeth way back when, he would have finished her off before she had any of the children that he now has to get rid of as well.

"Vincenzo is a desperate man," continued Brattini. "He told me that only if he pulls the trigger himself will he be sure that it will get done," Massimo went on. "And I keep encouraging him. As long as he thinks that I'll be happy to see you destroyed, he'll keep talking to me and I can keep a handle on what he is up to.

"Vincenzo also has a major money deal going on with Howard Ramsay and Yuri Latchman. They've let DeSalle know that they too would be happy if you were eliminated.

"So I've lined up a meeting with him next week in Ottawa to make a payoff to some Canadian politicians. I've decided to take him out then."

"Massimo," croaked Santino. "Do you think that's smart? It's been so long since either one of us took anyone out. Maybe you should bring in someone from Buffalo to do the job."

"It's not something a guy like me ever forgets how to do," Brattini answered forcefully. "And besides, now that I've told you the whole story, you're the only one I can trust, next to me, to take care of things if I fail. If anyone else gets involved, we might wind up with another war between our families.

"So for the sake of your wife and sons – my daughter and grandsons – we can't let that happen."

"Okay, stop the tape for a moment," said Johnny. He got up and walked over to the window. Angela came up behind him and put her arms around his waist and leaned her head against his back.

"I must admit I've heard this story once before...from Rebecca Sherman. But you know, it is one thing to have a story told to you by a third party, but it is entirely different listening to it in real time," he said. "I can't ever remember my father speaking to anyone in the tone of voice I'm now hearing. Sometimes he would soften up to Angela, but never to me. I wonder if my mother ever knew about this."

"She knew nothing," said Angela. "I would have known if she did. And from what I'm hearing, I guess Papa really did murder DeSalle."

"Just wait until we're done," Grant said quickly. "Then it will be clearer to all of you." He looked around the room and asked if anyone else wanted to speak.

The room was quiet. Then Grant removed the tape and turned to Elizabeth.

"Elizabeth, now you have to tell us the rest of the story in your own words."

She walked over to the bar and filled her glass with wine. Then she turned to look at the most important people in her life and spoke.

"Massimo was unable to kill DeSalle. I knew this when Rebecca spoke to Santino, and so I knew what Santino was going to ask her to do. I agree with Grant that it's important for all of you to know the words spoken between Rebecca and me after her visit with Santino. It will help you to understand why we did what we had to do.

"After Rebecca spoke to Santino that night, I decided to let it all hang out with her," she continued forcefully, "to let her know how I felt – before we figured out how to handle the crisis facing all of us."

As Elizabeth told her story, she looked as if she were in a far off place. It was clear to all that this was not something Elizabeth could ever forget.

"You know, I used to hate you," I said to Rebecca. She did not react.

"If you had been younger or prettier, I could have rationalized Santino's interest in you as the usual macho male sex drive," I went on.

"But I knew that it was more than that. He was always fascinated with your brains, your spirit and your intensity. I didn't know how to fight you.

"When we decided to return to Boston after the police and FBI investigations were over, we intended to leave any memories of the past behind us. Santino began to spend more time with our sons, taking an active role in their everyday lives. He seemed to have found some peace. Life has been good to us this past ten years Rebecca, and I will be forever grateful, not only to God, but to you."

"That's stretching it a bit isn't it?" she answered after a few moments, not bothering to hide the skepticism in her voice.

"Yes, it's true," I insisted. "You loved him enough to let him go, knowing that he would return to us, where he belonged. I admired you then, and I admire you even more now.

"Now, the past is over," I went on as forcefully as I could. "We have to move on with the task at hand."

"No!" Rebecca snapped at me as she stood up and walked over to the window, staring out at the stars for a few moments. Then she turned back with a very cold look in her eyes.

"Look Elizabeth, I'm so sorry for all the pain I've caused you, I truly am. But you can't get involved in what I have to do. This is business."

"But I'm already involved," I insisted. "So whatever you decide needs to be done, I intend to help. You can't do it alone."

Elizabeth paused to take sip of wine. "The two of us were sitting in the kitchen when Rebecca called Bob DeSalle," she told them. "She held the phone away from her ear so that I could hear their conversation. She gave him a story about his cover being blown and that if he wanted to settle any scores, he better come to Boston right away."

Elizabeth's face turned white. No one moved. They all knew she was somewhere else, deep inside a memory.

The doorbell rang right on time. I was sitting at Santino's bedside. I crossed myself as I got up from the chair and prayed to our Lord Jesus to forgive me for what I was about to do. I wanted Him to help me to live with the guilt that I knew I would have to carry for the rest of my life – but I had to save my sons.

"Hello Bingo," said Rebecca as she opened the front door. "Welcome to Boston."

"Give me your piece," I heard her say in a loud voice as they stepped into the elevator. "The guards will frisk you upstairs, but they won't touch me."

The silence lasted only seconds. I heard DeSalle yelling, "What the fuck?"

"Roberto Vincenzo! Morte! Carogna!" Rebecca answered him.

Three gun shots rang in the air.

The doors slid open on the fifth floor. I was waiting, wearing jeans and one of my son's lumber jackets. I reached out and took Rebecca's arm. She was white-faced and shaken. At first neither of us looked down at the body, but then I did and the words popped out of my mouth, "God damned dirty bastard."

We walked slowly back into the house and Rebecca stopped and put her hand on my shoulder. In a very quiet voice she said, "Elizabeth, Santino must never know how this job was done."

I wouldn't be surprised if he knew what you would do even before you did I thought.

"Don't worry," I told her. "He'll never know."

"Well, talk about revelations," said Peter as he got up and did a bit of stretching and bending. "I need a few minutes."

His wife Angela also got up and walked over to her brother Johnny. She put her arms around him for a moment before she turned to take Peter's hand.

"Well, at least Papa was innocent of this killing," she said. Then Peter turned to Elizabeth.

"Mama, I'd be lying if I didn't tell you that I'm shocked at your decision to participate in what we've just heard," he said. "If someone had told me this story I would probably have burst out laughing, thinking it was a joke. But obviously it's not a joke. I'll have to get my head around it...but not right now."

"Mama, I'm less shocked than Peter," said Matthew as he too got up and walked over to his mother. "I always knew that you knew more about what Papa was into than you let on. But, you and your friends all laboured under guilty delusions – delusions that their kids couldn't read, couldn't hear, couldn't see and most important, couldn't figure out.

"People do what they need to do to make it through the night. That understanding helps me in what I do and helps me to be less judgemental. You have a strength that I never appreciated until this moment. You made sure that all of us made it through the night, and, for what it's worth, you are still and will always be my special love."

Elizabeth's eyes were closed and she didn't respond or lift her head.

"So, my mother was a Mafia hit man, or should I say hit-lady," Lisa said in a quiet voice that was so cold. "Very nice. And what do I tell her grandson? Guess what Sam, Bubbie Rebecca shot some guy in the chest...in cold blood.

"And then, if that isn't enough my baby son, I have more news for you. A year later someone blew up her car with her in it. But don't let it bother you or affect your own life. Get over it."

"Lisa, it's not that simple," said Elizabeth as she tried to put her arms around her. Lisa pushed her away. "Your mother saved our lives – Peter, Matthew and me. Sure in hindsight it's easy to question decisions taken in moments of panic..."

"Panic?" snapped Lisa. "What panic? My mother didn't panic. She thought it out. She set it up. She didn't think twice about the repercussions. DeSalle had to be neutralized, and in her world that meant murder.

"And why did she have to do it herself?" she asked turning around to look at Johnny. "Your father and Santino had plenty of men who could have done it."

"Look Lisa, it is obvious that my father and Santino made a private arrangement when Santino was near death," Brattini said very softly, trying to hide his feelings of deep concern and affection for her from the others. "I'm sure that time was of the essence and knowing how things were back then, there was always the possibility of creating a turf war…again."

"Lisa!" Angela said forcefully, walking over to her. "DeSalle was my biological father because he raped my mother. He didn't know it and would no doubt have killed both Johnny and me if your mother hadn't stopped him. I have no intention of telling my daughters anything, nor do I really care about the genetics. My Papa was my love – and he loved me. That is all that matters. I don't care about anything else, and I strongly urge you not to tell Sam any of this. There will be nothing to gain. Trust me."

"I'm just as guilty as Rebecca," interjected Elizabeth. "We talked it through, and I helped her set him up – I knew what I was doing."

She looked over at Larry. His face was like a mask – hiding any emotion he was feeling.

"You didn't stand in front of a living person and shoot him dead," Lisa choked out.

"Let's not give DeSalle any principles that he didn't own" said Matthew as he walked over to Lisa. "Your mother's primary goal was to save her family – and luckily for us we were included. Whatever her sins, there is no doubt she has been forgiven."

"Right," snapped Lisa. "That's the same rationale you guys use when someone comes to you to confess – whether it is murder, child abuse or eating meat on Friday. You give them some miniscule repentance exercise and then forgive them. And when they come back six months later having murdered someone else, you forgive them again. Tell me Matts, did anyone in your organization ever give that some serious thought?"

"Good idea," Matthew answered, a smile filling his face. "How about writing me a report and I'll take it with me when I return to Rome tomorrow."

"I think I will, just to make sure that someone does," she answered, trying not to smile back at him. Everyone else was quiet.

"Well, here I am, the only Jewish princess present, surrounded by infidels," Lisa went on, her voice softening. "Just remember that your very own Jesus was once one of my people."

"He still is," laughed Matthew. "And you had better remember that these very same Catholic infidels will be sitting in *Shul* at Sam's Bar Mitzvah fighting off the urge to kneel and cross themselves."

Peter then turned to Grant. His face was a combination of sadness and anger when he started talking.

"In the tape, Brattini said that Yuri Latchman and Howard Ramsay encouraged DeSalle's actions. This isn't over is it? Mama helped Rebecca stop DeSalle, but Latchman and Ramsay still want us dead. That's why we're all here. That's why you say the family is in danger."

CHAPTER FOURTEEN

Grant and Larry looked around the room. They knew the time had come to begin asking Peter and Johnny for information. Elizabeth had done all she could. It was their turn.

Peter continued to speak, but this time more to himself than to the others, "I thought Yuri Latchman was my friend."

"I need you to share everything you know about Latchman with me," Larry said, smiling as he saw the grimace appear on Peter's face.

"I know, I know. But this isn't a movie. It is a life-risk. You already have our commitment that any information found relative to you or your business will be immune. Period. The information will only be used to nail Latchman, if he is a key player in this as we suspect that he is. And if we are right, then Ramsay is going down with him."

"Our agencies will not share any information with you," Larry continued. "You will have no input in what we do – but we need the routes he works, the cartels he supplies and his diamond connections. We need to make sure he hasn't contracted anyone else to help him do his dirty work."

"Wait!" said Peter. "You sound like you already know something."

"Yes, we do," answered Larry. "Our agent had a delightful conversation with some couriers nabbed at the Mexican – U.S. border, and they sang the name Latchman."

"Peter, you have no choice!" snapped Elizabeth as she walked over to face her son. "I believe Grant and Larry. I don't wish to live out my days looking over my shoulder or the shoulders of those I love waiting for the axe to fall. All you are being asked to do is give them information. Whatever happens after that is out of your hands. I have just given them evidence of my being an accessory to murder.

"If the suspicions about Latchman turn out to be true," she went on, "then he has been betraying you from day one. Maybe we will learn the reason why, maybe not. I don't care. I want it over. I've had enough. I promise you, as I once promised your father, that I will not raise the subject of what you do ever again."

Peter continued to stare at her in silence.

"If the only way that we can safeguard our family is for you to cooperate and share information that you already have, then you will share it! I am your mother! I insist on it! You will do it!"

The room was quiet. Peter didn't respond to his mother's outburst. He knew better than most how difficult it would be for him to defy her.

"I am not going to say anything until somebody tells me why Yuri Latchman would want to kill our family," Peter said. "Am I supposed to believe this just because Massimo Brattini said so, and so many years ago? And tell me Johnny, what do you know that we don't?"

Johnny knew that he was the only one who had the answers needed to get Peter to cooperate, but revealing them meant openly admitting the extent of their rivalry and potentially destroying his newest business venture. But then he thought, *Rebecca and I came to respect each other a long time ago. I owe this to her. And if anything ever happened to Lisa.* He stood up suddenly and spoke.

"Yuri Latchman wants your family dead, Peter, because he wants to take over DeLuca Industries. He always has, which is why my father knew he supported DeSalle's plan to murder the entire DeLuca family." Johnny paused for a moment and then continued, "Latchman also believes you murdered his uncle, Boris Latchman."

Peter DeLuca stood up and glared at Brattini. "I hardly know anything about Boris Latchman. I'd never even met him. All I know is that he lent my father money when he needed it."

Johnny nodded, knowing that Peter was telling the truth. "Sit down Peter, and let me explain." Johnny took a deep breath and continued,

"DeSalle had told me about the exchange between Santino DeLuca and Boris Latchman. So six months after taking over DeLuca's notes in exchange for giving him cash and credit, I paid Boris Latchman a visit."

"What can I do for you Mr. Brattini?" Latchman asked as he motioned for me to take a seat.

"It's what I can do for you, Mr. Latchman," I answered quietly with what I hoped was a pleasant smile on my face. "I understand that you're holding notes from the P&M Trust as collateral for some loans. I'd like to buy them from you."

Boris tried to hide his surprise. He seemed very shocked that I had this information.

"I knew how insidious the Mob could be, and I had heard that DeLuca and Brattini were arch enemies," he said, almost to himself. "Did DeSalle betray DeLuca?"

When I didn't answer, he stood up. "The notes are not for sale," he said quite forcefully. "And whoever told you that they were was misinformed. Now if you'll excuse me, I have another appointment."

I didn't move. Then I pulled a folded document out of my inside pocket. "This is the transfer of ownership for those notes," I said, ignoring Boris' icy stare. "As you can see, one million dollars in gold will be transferred to your Swiss account as soon as you sign this document."

Boris was laughing as he walked over to me, his eyes glaring.

"The P&M notes are worth close to six million dollars," he whispered menacingly. "Even if I was interested in selling them, which I am not, why would I discount them to you for only fifteen percent of their face value?"

"Because right now, gold in the Soviet Union is worth ten times its market value," I answered. "And I presume that is where you will use it – in the Volyus Trading Company. That is its correct name, isn't it? Diamonds and gold? Black market smuggling via Sierra Leone and Kiev? And as long as the Soviet government, especially Mr. Yeltsin, doesn't find out about your silent partner, you know, the Minister of Justice's wife, you should do just fine."

"Boris gave me the notes in the end. A week later, Boris Latchman was driving along I-95 near Palm Beach when he stopped behind a large truck apparently stalled on the road," Johnny summarized. "A larger transport truck speeding behind him rear-ended his car. He died instantly. Three days later Latchman's Bayfield Trust was taken over by a numbered company registered in the Turks & Caicos.

"DeSalle fed lies to Yuri Latchman so that he would believe that it was DeLuca who had arranged for his uncle's death. This reinforced Yuri's plan to destroy the DeLuca family, along with Rebecca Sherman. Latchman's association and apparent friendship with you Peter was just a deflection to keep everyone off guard. Murder and the takeover of DeLuca Enterprises was always his intention."

Peter DeLuca stood up and glared at Brattini. "You bastard. I've always suspected you took our notes from Boris, but I couldn't prove it.

"But you don't have it all. I know that Rebecca transferred the P&M money to Israel," Peter said, "and in order to do it, she had to have transferred P&M funds to Israel before Dad assigned the rest to Boris Latchman.

"The amount Rebecca transferred would have been about three million dollars sixteen years ago. How much is it worth today?" Peter asked.

"Well, it would depend on how it was invested," answered Johnny, forcing himself to look directly into Peter's eyes. "And I already know about that money. My father met with Rebecca shortly after Santino's death and tried to get her to return it to him."

"And I wonder what her answer was," piped in Matthew.

"Whatever happened back then, was then," Larry interjected. "Banking laws have changed – especially in Israel. If the P&M money Rebecca transferred is still in Israel, the only way the money could be transferred back from Israel to either Canada or the US would be through a ministerial or presidential order. And if the beneficiary is a Jew, then that would add lots of brownie points and be much easier to legitimize with Israel."

Larry and Grant made eye contact, and Grant's body language told Larry that they were both on the same page: the memos with P&M

listed beside Latchman and Ramsay's names now made sense. Larry took the two folded memos from the breast pocket of his jacket and laid them on the table for everybody to see.

"We discovered these memos during two recent drug-smuggling busts. It looks like Latchman and Ramsay want that P&M money," Larry explained.

"Who's Ramsay?" Lisa asked.

"The Deputy Minister of Justice," Grant answered.

"Ramsay must be using Yuri because he's Jewish," Peter said. "But how would Ramsay have known that Rebecca transferred some of the P&M notes?"

"Ladies and Matthew, I need to talk with Peter and the investigators alone for a moment," Johnny announced.

"Okay," Grant said in a strong voice. "We have lots of work to do and not too much time to do it. Larry and I can't thank you enough for agreeing to meet with us, especially you Elizabeth. Thankfully, your part in this meeting is now over. We'll meet you and the kids for dinner in about an hour."

"Larry, please join us for dinner when your meeting is over," said Elizabeth before she turned to leave. "It will mean a lot to me."

"Sure," mumbled Larry, stunned by Elizabeth's words. "Means a lot to me too."

Grant glanced over at his brother and gave him a quick wink, which he hoped no one else noticed. As the others were leaving, Matthew took Larry's arm.

"I need about ten minutes to speak to you when you're done," he said with a smile.

"No problem," answered Larry. "After all, what can be wrong with being in the company of a Vatican envoy?"

When the others had left the room, Larry and Grant sat down across the table from Peter and Johnny.

"Okay, Johnny," Larry began, "What do you have for us?"

Johnny hesitated for a moment. "I've been trying to get Rebecca's money back ever since she turned down my father's request. I saw

Latchman and Ramsay as a way to do it, so I told them about the P&M money in Israel."

"*You're* using Latchman and Ramsay to get the money," Peter said in outrage. "You know that those notes were originally assigned to Rebecca. Lisa is her heir, Johnny. If they need an heir in order to get that money, you've put Lisa in serious danger."

Oh god, what have I done, thought Johnny. *This was never supposed to involve Lisa.*

"Until today, we only knew that Latchman and Ramsay were up to something regarding the P&M Trust," Larry added. "But Johnny, this is your scheme. You know what this means, right?"

Johnny tried to keep his cool. "I have immunity in this room, remember? If I agree to help you, you keep me out of this investigation...and out of jail."

"If Ramsay and Latchman go to jail, you stay out," Larry replied. "But to make that happen, they'll need to believe you're still on their side."

"I can do that," he agreed, thinking only of Lisa.

"But why would Ramsay help? What's in it for him?" Peter asked. Then Peter went flush. *Latchman and I gave the documentation of Ramsay's payoffs – the pictures and negatives – to Rebecca, along with that video. And Latchman had been working against me that whole time! Fuck, fuck, oh fuck!*

"It's okay, Peter," Grant reassured him, seeing the panic in Peter's eyes. "We all know about the evidence against Ramsay that you and Latchman gave to Rebecca. Rebecca left it with me before she died. I gave copies to Johnny soon after, on Rebecca's request."

Peter shook his head, "I'd kill whoever I had to to get that video back if it were me in it. Those prostitutes, and that dog...." He let out a shudder.

"Listen," Grant interjected. "Rebecca is dead. It's one thing if Latchman and Ramsay are just trying to get their hands on the money she transferred to Israel, but if they are harbouring a mutual need for retribution, they only have her family to go after now."

"Does anyone besides me get the feeling that none of this is really happening?" asked Peter with a wry smile. "The cops and the family – sitting across from each other to jointly plan a party to end all parties."

"Peter, thirty years ago your father and I met in a motel room," said Grant. "We talked through a problem that we solved for both of us. I would have arrested him if I had the evidence I needed but I didn't. Despite that, I trusted him and he trusted me. I never dreamed I would be in a similar circumstance again."

"Between the four of us, I have no concerns," said Johnny. "But as for your associates in the FBI and RCMP, I have real concerns. So the responsibility for the protection of our interests will be yours, Larry. Once we have confirmation, Peter and I will do what we have to do...sooner rather than later. It will be over quickly if we don't have to watch our tails. Can we count on you?"

"Yes, can we?" added Peter as he stared intently at Larry.

"Yes, you can," answered Larry looking at Peter's green eyes, so much like those of Elizabeth. "Do what you have to do. Let me know only what you have to.

"And then we can all move on. But you know that we'll still keep trying to nail your asses while you guys continue trying to move faster than we can."

The men stood and shook hands. No more words were spoken. When Peter and Johnny had left the room, Larry turned to Grant.

"I really can't be a part of this group right now," he said. "Maybe when it's all over – but if I am seen here or a camera picks us up on the street, the repercussions are mind boggling. Tell Elizabeth…something. I'm going back to the hotel. I'm flying back to Toronto early in the morning. I'll touch base with you in a day or two."

The two brothers embraced and Larry turned and left through the den doors into the garden. He checked it out before pushing his way through the huge bushes to the street where his driver was waiting.

"Where to Boss?" asked Fabian as he jumped out to open the back door.

"Hotel," answered Larry. "And our flight leaves at nine in the morning so you better wake me at eight. Nice to have a private plane, eh? No line ups, etc., etc."

Fabian smiled. "Ya, for sure. By the way, I did a couple of drives around the street when you were inside – nothing – all clear, for now."

"Thanks for thinking of that," said Larry as he stretched his legs and closed his eyes. "I have more important things on my mind."

CHAPTER FIFTEEN

Sam was still playing one of his games on his iPad as Grant followed him and Lisa into the house after they had finished dinner at the Lobster House. Grant always used the guest bedroom on the main floor when he was in town, and he headed towards it with Sam right behind him.

"Hey Dad, check out this game," said Sam as he held up the "thing," as Grant always called it, for his father to look at. For the first time Grant noticed that Sam could almost reach his chin. In another year he might be taller than him.

Wow, he thought. *He's already as tall as Lisa.*

"Sam, you have school tomorrow," Lisa called from the kitchen. "This has been another late night. What do you want for lunch?"

Grant smiled. This was the closest he would ever be to domesticity and he welcomed the nice – no, more than nice – feeling that surrounded him. He loved being here, even when Isobel was still in residence. Lisa made him so comfortable and she always respected his privacy. It also gave him the opportunity to spend so much quality time with Sam, time that wasn't structured or dependant on a clock. Often the two of them just sat around watching TV or playing Scrabble; a game they both enjoyed.

Now that Isobel was gone, Lisa hung around the two of them more than usual. Grant didn't mind and assumed that she was getting over whatever it was that one got over when a relationship ended. He had decided long ago to make no judgements on Lisa's decisions. He never let any relationship of his get beyond the first stages of intimacy; he enjoyed companionship and shared fun and of course, sex, which, next to golf, was his favourite pastime. But even though Rebecca was dead she would always be a part of him, and Lisa and Sam were his living memory of her.

And then there was Jennifer White. Fire, madness, no inhibitions – that woman was incredible. She was passionate, fun, undemanding and so erotic. Her body was always receptive to being feasted upon, and as long as one could keep it up, the ecstasy continued. He had only known her for a couple of months, but Grant almost always got an erection when he thought of her.

But I really do love being here and relaxing, he thought. *No demands, no pressure. Sam is my treasure. And Lisa is just like a perfect sister – supportive, understanding and easy to be with.*

"Night Dad," said Sam as he came into his room wearing his new rock band PJs. Elizabeth had picked them up in New York and Sam loved them. "Will you be here tomorrow when I come home from school?"

"Maybe," answered Grant. "I think Uncle Matt wants to speak to me and if there's nothing else, I'll probably go back to Florida the day after tomorrow. But I did speak to Kevin and he says 'hi bro' and wanted me to tell you that he's making another record on his iPad."

Sam smiled. "That's great. I can't wait to see him.

"I'm still working on an interesting clue in my fact-checking course. Actually, if what I've uncovered is really an actual fact as it seems to be, it'll be incredible."

"Well that sounds mysterious," said Grant. "I can't wait to hear all the details. And is Rhonda still working with you?"

Sam's faced turned red as he nodded to his father and then trotted off for bed.

"Okay," said Lisa as she walked into Grant's room. "I'm ready for the lecture." She sat down on the chair next to the bed and gave him a phony smile.

"No lecture," answered Grant ignoring her facial expressions. "But I do think it's time you accepted the past for what it is – just that – the past. None of us can go back and change anything now. And that expression, 'hindsight is 20/20' was never more relevant than it is right now."

She said nothing and kept her big brown eyes focused on his.

"Just think again about how Elizabeth's sons must feel," Grant went on. "Forget Matthew for the moment. He's a man of God, and they can always find a rationale for any behaviour – but Peter? It has to be a real mind-blower for him to learn that his mother had a hand in the very action that he deals with all the time. Drug deals gone bad, lost shipments, millions of dollars in cash – and the probable betrayal by his associate. It sounds like an old movie script."

When he got no response from Lisa, Grant continued. "Until today, I wasn't fully aware of how involved Elizabeth was with Rebecca's activities, especially during the final year of Santino's life. I ignored the signs – probably because I didn't really want to know. But what does that all mean now?

"The end result was the tragic and untimely death of your mother. But the other reality is that the rest of you – the children and now grandchildren have lived and lived well. Up until now, you've all moved ahead with your lives with no fear or danger. Or at least we didn't know about any danger. But there is danger now – real danger – and it has to be eliminated once and for all.

"So get over it and move on Lisa," he went on forcefully. "You have a great career, you are the mother of a fabulous son that I am happy to take a lot of credit for, you are free of an unwanted relationship and you are beautiful. Go for it!"

Why did I just throw in "beautiful" to a conversation about murder and money? thought Grant.

He called me beautiful. I like that, thought Lisa as she smiled at him.

"Now, let's talk about Isobel," said Grant. "Sam simply said that 'Madame le Docteur' has left. I just want to know that you're okay with it."

When Lisa didn't answer Grant couldn't resist saying what had been in his head for years. "You know, I never could figure out why you turned to a woman."

Again, silence. So he continued on. *Let the chips fall where they may.*

"Even though I was drunk and in a lot of pain on that night of infamy between us, I still remember one or two important details."

"Oh, and what would those details be?" asked Lisa, her face now a mask.

"Well, certain parts of you were as they should be in such a circumstance."

"Speak English Grant," she smirked. "I have no idea what you're talking about."

"Your nipples were hard before I put my lips to them, and you were very wet where you're supposed to be when you're anticipating a hard visitor."

Lisa started to laugh. "I can't believe the way you've just described our wild and insane FUCK! What message are you really trying to send me?"

"Actually, I don't know," answered Grant, feeling like a jerk. "I don't even know why I brought it up now."

"Well, I think it's time for me to tell you the truth," said Lisa as she pulled the chair over to sit right in front of Grant.

"I wasn't drunk at all that night. In fact, I planned to get you into bed with me when I called you, though I was already crying before I did." Grant froze and his eyes narrowed as he stared at Lisa.

"I was really mad at my mother," she continued, her voice still strong, "mad at her for ignoring me when I was young; mad at her for being so involved with the Mob despite her saying it's just business; and really mad at her for dying and leaving me alone. So, I decided to punish her. And I knew what would bother her the most – sex with you, the man she loved.

"So I planned to seduce you on the chance that there might be another life somewhere and she would see what I was doing and that she would be hurt. Then I could forget her and move on."

Grant didn't react or take his eyes off Lisa's face. *Holy fucking shit! Can this be real?*

"Of course, you were not the first man I had sex with. But oh boy, even drunk, were you ever good.

"Then, when I woke up that morning, you were gone – not even a goodbye poem or note," she giggled.

"And almost immediately I regretted my insane rationale for what I'd done. But I wasn't sorry for the actual 'it' – never. And looking back, and even confessing to you now, I'm glad we did it – of course we have Sam – but I also have a special place to visit when I'm down."

Grant stood up and walked over to the window. *I'm really stunned – all those years of guilt.* He was having trouble digesting what Lisa had just told him.

"Isobel offered me a lot of comfort when I was most vulnerable," Lisa continued. "She kept me balanced; and she loved me. I enjoyed the sex we shared – never underestimate the pleasure of oral sex with a woman. As far as I knew, she was happy with the relationship we had.

"After five years, when Sam was ready for nursery school, I started to have second thoughts. We were in an easy routine, and I kept pushing any doubts out of my head. Your presence in Sam's life made it work even better. And Isobel knew that I wasn't there, really, as I had once been. But easy routines are hard to change if there's no other option or driving force.

"The last three months have become the driving force, and she left three weeks ago. We spoke briefly about some joint commitments, and I think she's as relieved as I am that it's over. So that's the story."

"Pardon me if I don't have a quick commentary for you right now," said Grant as he continued looking out the window. "I'll admit I'm in a bit of a shock. It's nice to hear how much the world revolved around you and what you wanted with little thought about the rest of us, or the repercussions.

"Anyhow, I'm going back to Florida tomorrow, and we'll talk again once I digest all of this."

"Sounds good," said Lisa as she got up and walked towards the door. *Oh my god. Don't let him see how embarrassed I am. Why did I tell him? What if he hates me?*

"I have a photo shoot next week on Hutchinson Island which is near you," said Lisa. "It should last about two days. Elizabeth is moving in here while I'm gone. Will I still be welcome to stay on the houseboat?"

"If I didn't like you so much, I would be pretty ticked off at your question," Grant snapped as he turned from the window to look at her. "So I'll pretend I didn't hear it.

"Keep in touch and confirm your arrival time at Orlando. I'll have someone pick you up."

"Thanks, but that won't be necessary," answered Lisa with a tentative smile on her face. "The magazine is responsible for moving me from place to place. But I will call you as soon I arrive."

CHAPTER SIXTEEN

Shit! I forgot to speak to Matthew before I left the town house, thought Larry as he poured himself a Scotch on ice. He looked at the clock on his laptop – ten thirty – the "group" must have finished dinner by now. He hesitated about calling Elizabeth's house where Matthew was staying, but he also sensed that Matthew must have something important to tell him. Then there was a knock on his door.

He took his gun out of the holster hanging over the bed frame and held it behind his back as he walked over to the door and opened it.

"Elizabeth! What are you doing here? How did you know where I was staying?"

"Gee, those very same words sound kind of familiar," she answered with a smile. "How long has it been since I asked them of you? It seems like only yesterday."

He reached out and yanked her into the room. She pretended to ignore the gun he quickly put on the table. She smiled as he took her face in his hands and stared into her eyes.

"Let's not speak, at least not for a while," she said as she put her arms around his neck. "I'm hoping you won't need a road map to remember."

"Remember?" he asked. "Since I first met you, not one day has passed in my life that you haven't been there." He leaned over and kissed her, running his tongue inside her lips until she did the same to him.

She moved her hand from his back to his waist and down from there.

"Oh, I'm so glad," she mumbled against his lips as her hand stayed pressed against his hard penis. "I was so scared that you wouldn't want me the way you once did."

He burst out laughing. "Want you? Are you insane? Get out of your clothes Elizabeth!" he said as he pulled her towards the bedroom, "and no more talking."

For the next several hours, in between short naps, they shared an intense, intimate and loving sexual encounter that writers have tried to describe in their novels since the beginning of time. Words of love were spoken; lips and tongues explored every part of their bodies that could respond; he penetrated and exploded inside her. But he also loved having her sit on his penis and rotate her hips as he watched her eyes glaze over before she had another orgasm.

He didn't hear the phone ringing until Elizabeth started climbing over his body to reach it. He wrapped his arm around her waist and picked it up. The clock read eight thirty in the morning.

"Sorry Fabian, I slept in," mumbled Larry as his eyes moved from Elizabeth's incredible green eyes down to her breasts. She stretched and smiled at him. "Call the airport and let them know we'll be delayed...maybe two hours."

"Sorry buddy, it's not Fabian, it's me," said Grant over the phone. "There's now a bit of a glitch. Fabian has delayed your flight at my request. You and I need to meet with Matthew. We can meet you at your hotel in twenty minutes."

"Umm," mumbled Larry.

"I guess you aren't alone," said Grant. "Well, what do you want to do?"

"Come on over in half an hour," answered Larry. "We can have coffee and bagels in the hotel's coffee shop."

"Well," huffed Elizabeth, pretending to be insulted when he hung up the phone and started to climb out of the bed. "I can see that I have served my purpose. I'm just a body to you, nothing more than that. And now that you've had your fill, you're leaving me."

"I won't even try to verbalize how much I love you, you wild woman," said Larry. "Just stay here while I meet with Grant and

Matthew. I have no idea what this is about but I'm sure it won't take long. And then we can have a rehearsal."

"A rehearsal? A rehearsal for what?" she laughed.

"The rest of our lives, together," he answered nibbling her lips. "I will never let you get away from me again."

Matthew and Grant were already eating when Larry sat down opposite them. After ordering a coffee and a poached egg, he looked at the two of them.

"So, what's up?" he asked.

"Did you at least order some room service for my mother so she doesn't go hungry?" asked Matthew, trying to keep a straight face.

For the first time since he was a little boy, Larry felt his face turn red as he looked down. He was actually mortified. And of course, good old Grant did his, "ha, you're caught!" routine.

"Sorry Larry," said Matthew after a few minutes when he realized just how genuinely embarrassed Larry was. "We have all known about you and Mama since once upon a time when she was working as a designer. And it has been kind of cute watching the two of you pretending not to notice each other these past few weeks – considering your advancing years."

"Hey, watch it!" snapped Larry as he poked Matthew's arm.

"Yah, watch it!" piped up Grant.

The relief Larry now felt was exhilarating.

"Well, I'm glad we had a fun start to this conversation," said Matthew. "I'm not sure how you'll feel about the rest of it."

When Grant put his arm on his shoulder, Larry knew a bomb was coming.

"As you know, my work in the Vatican focuses on finance and administration as well as some other things," Matthew began. "Part of my job is to follow up on the abuse allegations by the Church's representatives, usually priests, between 1945 and 2010. That includes orphanages."

Larry froze. Grant kept his arm where it was as Matthew went on.

"Three weeks ago I opened a new file – the Brothers of St. John Orphanage, founded in 1935 and closed in 1970. In those years, orphanages were supposed to be safe havens so no one at that time ever dreamed they were in fact hell holes.

"Vatican staff is responsible for going through all the entries of these institutions: arrivals, departures and deaths. There were rarely any departures and unfortunately, not all deaths were recorded. Sadly we now know why.

"As well, anything that looked questionable was to be sent to me. Two weeks ago one of our investigators who happens to be a novice nun – Sister Jacinta, from Thailand – found a note pinned under a message board that was in a box of old stuff."

"Oh God," whispered Larry. "It was about me, wasn't it?"

"It was a query dated December, 1969," answered Matthew as he locked eyes with Larry. "It was from a woman who said she had left her son at the orphanage four years earlier and now wanted him back. She gave her name as Lyla Leone and left a call-back number. As soon as I saw it I knew. The date matched the date of your arrival, and there were no others for three or more months. So I put Sister Jacinta on it to try and track Lyla Leone down, and with the internet tools available today, she found her. She's alive and she lives in Toronto. How ironic is that? The file says she was nineteen years old when she left her child, making her fourteen when she actually gave birth."

Larry said nothing. He was overwhelmed with joy, rage and frustration, all combined into one emotional roller coaster.

"Larry," Matthew went on, "I'm sure you can get your guys to track down her exact location very quickly. However, I would urge you, at this point in time, to ask yourself if you should really do that. Do you want to know? What if? She obviously cared enough to come back – she obviously didn't plan to permanently abandon you – that has to be a great consolation for you. But she might have made a new life for herself. Will you still be welcome in it?"

Larry was staring at Matthew and couldn't speak. *She didn't abandon me. She came back.*

"Anyhow, it's your call. Here are the notes," continued Matthew, "along with the old file and the information that Sister Jacinta compiled.

"Larry, whatever you decide to do, our prayers are with you. No one but the three of us knows of our meeting today. The decision on any next steps is yours alone. I'm leaving for Rome in about an hour. I won't be back in Boston until a few days before Sam's bar mitzvah so if you need to reach me, for any reason, this is my private line, day or night."

Larry was still silent. Grant patted his shoulder and then turned and whispered his thanks to Matthew.

"Go in peace, both of you," said Matthew when they all stood up to leave. He then made the sign of the cross on each of their foreheads. "May our Lord Jesus bless you both and keep you close to his heart. I am honoured to be your friend."

Grant and Larry walked out of the coffee shop and out to the parkette next to the hotel's main entrance. They sat down on the first bench and stared at the traffic in silence.

Finally, Larry said, "I'm going to find her. Then I'll decide if I go and see her. I'm not sure what I will say or do, but I need you to be with me."

"I will," answered Grant. "You're my brother."

"Elizabeth, my mother's been found!" shouted Larry as he walked into the bedroom. Elizabeth jolted up in the bed and a big smile filled her face. "Matthew was the key. He figured it out!"

"What can you tell me?" she asked as she got up with the sheet wrapped around her body.

"Nothing much, yet," he answered with a half smile, half frown on his face. "She lives in Toronto. Isn't that unbelievable?

"Grant has put his people on finding her exact location and has changed some of his appointments so he can come with me. I'll have to make some schedule changes myself, but hopefully we'll find her and get to her in a day or two.

"She tried to get me back," Larry went on. "All these years I thought she had abandoned me. I tried never to think about her, but sometimes her face would appear in my mind, usually when I was trying to sleep or when I was in Church and, of course, when Meghan was born.

"I'm not going to say anything to Meghan, not yet," mumbled Larry almost to himself. "I'll tell her about it when she joins me here before we go to Sam's bar mitzvah. That's seven weeks away and I should know all the details by then."

"What can I do to help you my darling?" asked Elizabeth as she put her arms around Larry's chest. "Count on me for anything you need."

"I'll tell you about the greatest gift you have given me, and I'm sure to many others," murmured Larry in her ear as his arms circled her sheet wrapped body. "It's your son, Matthew. There are no adequate words to describe the comfort and confidence I now have because of him. He is, in my opinion, the living embodiment of the message Christ hoped to pass along to the world. Love, caring, comfort and, most importantly, trust. Both you and Santino, together, had a part in him becoming the man, and the priest he is today. So don't underestimate it. And for sure don't forget it."

"What a comfort your words are to me, especially now," said Elizabeth as tears began falling. "I love you."

CHAPTER SEVENTEEN

Toronto, Ontario.

Mrs. Richard (Monica) Whitehead IV, a.k.a. FBI undercover agent Jennie White, walked briskly along Yorkville Avenue towards Avenue Road. She was heading towards the Granite Health Spa, a very private establishment for women. It offered the usual amenities of high-priced spas with one added bonus.

Its owner was a woman named Madame Heather Leopold, a.k.a. Lyla Leone – former teen prostitute and the biological mother of Larry Lyons. This was an unofficial exercise – a favour to her friend Larry – one that she hoped would also earn her brownie points with his brother Grant.

Oh, what a hunk he is, thought Jennie as she remembered last night's exercise with him in her Jacuzzi. For the first time in her life, Jennie was actually thinking about a long-term relationship. But first the matter at hand.

Lyla Leone had lived a colourful life and was a very skilled pleasure giver. Her first sexual experience happened when she was eight years old; her drunken mother never noticed how her live-in boyfriend used to hold one hand over Lyla's mouth to keep her quiet as he used his other hand to slip between her legs. When he penetrated her and Lyla cried out, her mother just turned her head the other way.

By the time she was twelve years old, Lyla decided that, since girls only had one purpose, namely to service guys, she would make it work for her.

So she left the shack in Northern Ontario where she had been born and abused and started a life on her own. When she became pregnant at age thirteen because she had no idea about birth control and the complicated inner workings of a woman's body, she was shocked. Her little boy was born in 1960 – he was the only person she would ever love. She spent five years trying to look after him properly and earn enough money to move into a proper home, but she couldn't do it. So she rationalized that if Larry could be looked after for just a year or two, she could earn enough money for the two of them to start over again. When she left him at the orphanage she promised to come back and get him. Four years later she tried to do just that, but she was told that he had died of pneumonia. Her pain was so overwhelming that she vowed to put her little boy's memory away forever. Sometimes she succeeded, sometimes she didn't.

Lyla spent the next years honing her skills. In fact, her most recent long-term client had appreciated her services so much that two years ago he bought her the Spa with her promise that she would learn to run it in a successful way. He also wanted her to have a pension of sorts and not to end her days giving blow jobs for five dollars each. It was a lucky break for Lyla and she grabbed it.

The Spa was a front for women in the market for young men, or at least men who could function sexually with much older women. Jennie knew this because she had talked up the subject of the Spa with Gina, the hairstylist in the Yorkville Hotel salon where Jennie was having her own hair done.

Gina was one of the referral agents used by the Spa to let the older women of means know of its existence. Or in plain English, any woman with cash, lots of it, could spend time in bed with a man with all the right parts and all the right moves. No embarrassment for the ladies – they paid, then got laid. And of course Gina got a fifty dollar referral fee. So far this month she had made over three hundred fifty dollars in cash.

"Why shouldn't a woman have the same options as a man?" asked Gina as she finished blow-drying the hair of Mrs. Richard Whitehead, IV. "Hookers, massage parlours, brothels and singles bars have always been okay for men. So what does a woman over fifty, usually over sixty do when she has become invisible to men but still wants to fuck? One day she's desirable and the next – it's all over, lady. She's told that she's too old. But her parts are still working and her juices still run when she thinks about a man's hard-on. She worries that when her breasts hang down to her waist will he also sag when he sees her naked body? Men seek out young and gorgeous bodies – that seems to be a given and perfectly acceptable. Being older doesn't really hold them back because it's only one part of them that has to get hard and stay hard. And now with the magic pills, their cocks can work even past their prime.

"But what about a woman? It's still a man's world – that's the way it is. They often pay for what they want...and need, so why can't a woman? "A good personality? Ha, in your dreams. Money is the great equalizer, and those that have it can get what they want."

"Well," answered Jennie. "I agree, and I'd love to try it but I'd be so scared of being caught by the police or having my picture taken or something like that. Is it illegal for a woman to hire a guy? The same as it is for a man to hire a prostitute?"

"Well, I'm not sure," answered Gina. "But I can certainly arrange for you to speak with Madame Leopold. She'll be able to answer your questions."

"Yes, can I help you?" said the receptionist as Jennie walked through the double glass doors of the Granite Health Spa.

"Yes, thank you," answered Jennie in her English accent. "I have a meeting with Madame Leopold."

"Welcome Mrs. Whitehead," said a stunning gray-haired woman dressed in a Ralph Lauren navy suit as Jennie got off the elevator. "It is a pleasure to welcome you to our Spa."

Lyla was slim, her hair was a stunning shade of salt and pepper and she was probably five foot six. She had the brightest eyes along with a smile that could easily be described as a million-dollar look. Jennie had to keep reminding herself of why she was here.

After a ten-minute tour of the Spa and all its services, Lyla took Jennie into her office. It was painted a single colour: gunmetal gray. Light oak floors, large uncovered windows, two gray leather couches and four gray leather chairs, a large bar, also done in gunmetal gray marble with a full-mirrored bar and what looked like a bookcase–TV–video cabinet with bookshelves filled with hardcover books. There were several Chagall prints on the walls.

"You don't look like a woman who needs to use my specialized services," said Lyla after pouring Jennie and herself a glass of Merlot. "Most of my clients are older than you."

"You're very kind," answered Jennie, her mind racing towards the right answer. "But my husband is no longer sexually active. In fact, he can't function at all. And I want to have sex, but I can't afford to be indiscreet and risk having someone tell my husband. I count on him for so much and the honest truth is a simple one – I can't afford to have him turn against me."

"Well, of course we are not in the prostitution business," smiled Lyla. "That would be illegal. We like to think of ourselves as matchmakers – specialized for sure – but still simply matchmakers. So after you and I have a frank and honest discussion about your wants and needs, we come to an agreement on a membership fee, payable in full once every year, and that is it. We then bring you together with friends of both sexes, and you choose whose company you wish to share."

"Oh, that sounds fine," said Jennie. "What are the membership fees?"

"They start at eighteen thousand, but it depends on your specific program plans; some members pay as much as seventy-five thousand."

Jennie had to take a breath and keep her eyes focused on the Chagalls or she would have burst out laughing.

"Well, thank you very much Madame Leopold," said Jennie. "This Spa could be just the answer I've been looking for. How do I reach you?"

"Leave a message on our machine Mrs. Whitehead," Lyla answered with a wide smile. "I'll get back to you within an hour."

Jennie, Grant and Larry were sitting in the bar of the Four Seasons Hotel where Jennie had been staying during the ongoing INSETs investigation. Larry had little colour in his face after listening to Jennie's report and he said nothing when she was finished.

"Look Larry," said Grant as he finished his drink. "Madame Leone is obviously way ahead of the crime game; she isn't charging fees for service, she's charging a mile-high membership fee to the clients and then paying the men herself. It's a loophole but it'll work. And I'm sure that all the women are well serviced, and that all the men they use are also well hung, and skilled – or at least have access to a pill if they need an extra kick to get it up."

"No kidding, Grant," laughed Jennie. "One of her clients, the one who pays seventy-five thousand a year, is over eighty years old. Good for her!"

Both Larry and Grant raised their eyebrows and tried not to laugh.

"Anyhow Larry, the next step is yours and yours alone," said Grant. "Matthew was right when he raised the question of whether you would actually want to pursue this. Give it some thought. Call me if you need me. Otherwise I'm going back to Florida tomorrow. I've let my business sit in limbo for too long.

"And remember: I'm the one who is to maintain direct contact with Peter and Johnny. You stay far back and I'll keep you posted."

"Okay, thanks," said Larry. "I don't know what I'm going to do about my mother. I'll let you know when I know."

CHAPTER EIGHTEEN

Jennie started taking off her clothes as soon as they got into her room. And true to form, Grant was immediately hard. There was silence as they stroked, licked and nibbled each other's bodies on their way to the edge of the bed. Grant sat down and Jennie got down on her knees and closed her lips around the tip of Grant's penis. He put his hands on the back of her head and pushed himself deep into her mouth. He thought his head would blow off with the intensity of his orgasm.

Later, much later when the two of them were stretched out in the Jacuzzi sipping on some wine, their conversation turned to business mostly at Grant's instigation.

"What the hell does '3rd hole' mean?" he asked. "I'm a golfer so that's the first thought that enters my head. But what can it mean in relation to murder, money laundering and illegal diamond shipments? And there are thousands of golf courses, and they all have #3 holes."

"Maybe it isn't a golf hole," answered Jennie. "Could be a diamond mine shaft – their holes are numbered. Could be a border entry – in Arizona they identify the breaks in the fence by hole numbers. What about a smuggling entry?"

"Not in this case," answered Grant. "We already know that Latchman is using aboriginals, primarily Mohawks. So once he gets whatever it is into either country it can be transported across the border without any hassles."

"Lantinos and his friends at the CIA think it is diamonds covering up terrorist tracks," Jennie said as she reached over and put her wine glass on the floor. "I'm still not sure they aren't overreacting. It's almost too small, too amateurish for me to buy into that, yet."

Then she turned on her back and stretched her body until she was on top of Grant with her legs opened around his shoulders.

He looked at her face with a smile before he looked at the vagina now being eased towards his mouth.

"I hate to change the subject," she whispered. "But equality is the name of the game. I do you, you do me. Isn't that how it works?"

There's nothing like the feeling of a man's tongue rolling over my clit, thought Jennie as she tightened her legs around Grant's shoulders and arched her back. She began shuddering in ecstasy as she put her hands on the side of the Jacuzzi and tried not to drown.

Twenty minutes later they were both wrapped in the individual robes that the hotel provided nibbling on the chips they found in the hotel room's mini-refrigerator. Grant continued talking about the project.

"Nailing Latchman would be great," said Grant as he chomped away. "But getting Ramsay would be a real coup. He's right up there with access to anything the prime minister sees."

Only Grant knew that there was more involved than just getting Ramsay. It was more about who Ramsay was trying to get – how much he knew about the stuff Rebecca had on him and what he believed was still out there. When Grant had given Brattini the porno tape years ago he had expected him to handle it. But Ramsay was still here. *Is it possible that Brattini is in cahoots with Ramsay? There isn't a doubt in my mind that Lisa and Sam are at risk. Why and how I am not yet sure? But as long as Ramsay is still politically active, the danger to them is getting closer.*

Grant chose not to share any of this with Jennifer fearing that the information could diminish the global perspective of Ramsay and Latchman in her mind, turning it into a personal vendetta. He had the same concerns about Bob Lantinos' reaction. So this was going to remain between him and Larry.

"I'm going back to Florida tomorrow," Grant said as he picked up the room service menu. "Larry is handling his mother on his own. And what an incredible story that is."

"Incredible isn't the ONLY right word," said Jennie. "Add mind-blowing, glorious, fairytale, wow! And who is going to tell Elizabeth that her pseudo mother-in-law is only a few years older than she is?"

"Hey, how did you know about Elizabeth?" asked Grant, turning to look into her eyes. "I never mentioned it."

Oh shit! I slipped. Think you idiot! You can't mention Bartoli and his comments to Lantinos.

"Oh come on Grant," she snapped. "You guys may be blind but we girls aren't. The chemistry between the two of them is hardly too obvious."

"Yeah, I guess you're right," smiled Grant. *Whew*, she thought. *There's nothing like a good offense to offset a lousy defence.*

"I'll talk to Lisa about it when I get home," he said. "She's close to Elizabeth. She'll know what to do or at least what to tell Larry to do."

"Oh, is Lisa in Florida?" asked Jennie as her heart sank.

"Yes, she has a photo shoot about ten minutes away from the houseboat. She always stays there if she's close by."

Jennie was now at a loss as to her next move. It had been an incredible time of sex and real affection and fun between the two of them. She had hoped that Grant was feeling the same. She didn't want it to end. For the first time in her life she was looking at a long-term relationship – and it was Grant she wanted it to be with. *Oh well, take a shot and see how it goes.*

"You know Grant, I've really enjoyed sharing so much with you these last few weeks," she said, *Put a big smile on your face just in case he freezes. Then you can make it light.*

"Me too," he answered without looking up from some notes he had just taken out of his wallet.

Well, that went over like a lead balloon.

"I'm curious," she continued. "Have you had a serious relationship in the past ten years?"

"No, I'm not interested," he answered without lifting his head. "I have my sons Kevin and Sam who are really my world. And of course, I have an excellent relationship with Sam's mother. She and I are good friends. So I'm very content with the domestic part of my life and I wouldn't let anything screw that up."

Well, that little speech just told me to wake up and move on.

"Okay," said Jennie. "What's our next step?"

"I expect some movement on the part of Latchman in the next week or two," Grant answered. "He's had two diamond shipments screwed up so whoever he partners with can't be happy. He'll have to take more risks this time around – and we'll be ready."

CHAPTER NINETEEN

This was the third day that Larry was sitting on a bench closest to the sidewalk on Yorkville Avenue waiting for Lyla Leone to walk by on her way to or from the Spa. He was wearing dark glasses, a golf hat and a golf shirt that he changed every time he went to sit there so she wouldn't notice him. He knew that his behaviour was not professional and he was having a hard time staying focused on his job. At first glance, there was nothing about her that he recognized or that seemed familiar. Luckily his office on Bay Street was only a ten minute walk away and he went back there in between vigils.

All he could think of was the mother he had once known who always had a hug and a kiss for him, who always told him how special he was, who always told him how much she loved him – and whom he hadn't seen since he was five years old.

Elizabeth had offered to come to Toronto with him, but he insisted that she stay in Boston to take care of Sam as she had promised Lisa. Besides, Larry wanted to deal with this on his own. He had not bothered to read his staff's report on what she had done before that. He didn't really care; it wasn't going to change anything.

"What does it matter?" I asked Grant, who was sitting next to me just after I saw my mother for the first time, walking from Aroma Coffee Bar towards her Spa. She apparently had a regular daily routine: breakfast at Pusateri, lunch at Il Posto, dinner at One; everything in the same block, no changes. She walked back and forth

three times a day, and then returned to her condo until the next day when it started again.

"Her past can't be anything I need to know or anything that will make a difference," I continued. "I have to reconcile all of this and decide if I want to confront her face to face. The fact that she eventually tried to come back for me makes such a difference. All the years that I didn't know...I assumed that she didn't care about me at all.

"But I also have to consider Matthew's words. Maybe it will disrupt her life knowing that I was alive all these years when she believed I was dead.

"So I really need to work this through on my own bro," he continued. "So go back to Florida and do what you have to do. We still have to make sure that the Peter and Johnny matter is put to bed before Sam's bar mitzvah. I'll keep you posted."

On the fourth morning, Madame Leopold made a sudden ninety-degree turn and walked right up to Larry sitting on the bench. It happened so fast that he was unprepared and froze. All his years of undercover and investigative experience had just gone out the window.

She smiled broadly at him. "Is there something I can do for you?" she asked.

That's my Mom! His thoughts were suddenly in chaos. Her smile – there was only one smile that had filled his head for all these years. *It's really her! Okay Larry, get a handle on it or you'll start crying like a baby. Take a deep breath.*

"Who are you?" she asked. "And why are you so interested in me?"

"You're pretty observant," he answered without thinking. "Ever think about joining the police department?"

She burst out laughing again. *It's her! It's her!*

"Well, the good news is that I was never concerned about who you might be," she answered. "But I thought that if you wanted to become one of my team, you would have come to the Spa directly. So what's the story? I'm dying to know."

Larry stood up. He looked down at her sparkling eyes and put his hands on her shoulders.

"Hi Mom," he whispered. "It's me, Larry. I've finally found you. We have lots to talk about." Then he quickly folded her now stiffened body into his arms and held her as close as he could.

She pulled her head back and stared at him. Then she started to cry, suddenly and quite visibly and her arms went around his neck. She kept lifting her head to look at him.

"My baby, my baby!" she sobbed looking into his eyes. "They told me you were dead!" And then, a torrent of sobs really overwhelmed her. People walking along the street started to slow down and stare.

"Hey, someone might think I'm hurting you and call the cops" whispered Larry. "Come on, let's go to my house. It's just around the corner." He put his arm around her shoulder and eased her as close to his body as was possible. Then the two of them turned and walked slowly and silently towards Larry's town house which was only ten minutes away.

Once inside, Larry broke down completely and made no effort to control his emotions. Lyla was also sobbing as she kept clinging to him.

Fifteen minutes later, Lyla's sobs had settled down to an occasional squeak and Larry was still fighting to get back in control. Then Lyla decided to have a glass of wine.

"Nice bar you have," she said as she looked it over, "and with some very good wines. You must have inherited my good taste." That brought out the famous Larry Lyons smile and his sobs ended.

"I would like to just sit here and look at you while you tell me everything about what you have done with your life," Lyla continued as she took his hand. "I know that listening to you will make me so proud and happy."

"How do you know that?" asked Larry still wiping tears from his eyes. He had a box of Kleenex right next to him on the couch.

"The way you look, the obvious way you live," she answered. "Now that I'm feeling better, we can talk."

Two hours later mother and son were both exhausted. Larry had taken his mother through his life to date and all the roads he had travelled. He left out the part about the abuse at the orphanage but included how important Grant and the late Brian and Janet Teasdale were in his life. He didn't mention Meghan…or Elizabeth.

"You haven't asked me anything," said Lyla. "And I appreciate that. It is also a statement about your instincts and sensitivity that reinforces my pride in you. I want us to move forward from this day only. My past is just that – the past. I did what I had to do. I'm not sorry and I'm not ashamed. I wish someone had loved me as much as I loved you. But no one ever did.

"I assume that you know what my Spa is all about," she continued. "It's actually quite important to me. I've covered my tracks and there's no illegality in its operation. I really believe that the positive effects women of a certain age enjoy as a result of what I do enhance and expand their lives and perhaps even improve their health. So there will be no discussion about that, at least not for a while.

"And now, I'm really tired," she said, smiling at him. "I'd prefer to go to my own place and do some revitalization. Then I'll have to check in at the Spa and make sure everything is working well."

"Good," said Larry as he got up and took his cellphone out of his pocket. "I also need the rest of the day to get myself functional again and to check in with the office. Shall we plan on an intimate dinner, just you and me? And what fun we're going to have if someone asks you who I am."

Lyla burst out laughing. "Oh, you are divine!" she gasped. "I am so lucky. Now what would you like to call me? Madame? Lady Leopold? Or, how about just plain Mom?"

"Mom," Larry said as he started tapping on the screen. "I forgot to tell you something, something very important."

Lyla looked up at him.

"You have a granddaughter," he said with a wide grin. "Her name is Meghan. She's a professor at McGill University in Montreal, and I am so proud to be able to introduce her to you."

Lyla's eyes opened wide and her mouth dropped as Larry punched in numbers on his cellphone.

"Meghan! Hi baby girl! Yes, I am so fine. Guess what? I finally found your grandmother. Yes, she's right here with me. Okay, hold on, I'm handing her the phone."

CHAPTER TWENTY

Pte. St. Lucie, Florida.

Grant was surprised to see that Lisa's luggage was still in the spare bedroom when he finally got home at noon. He thought she was here for only a two-day photo shoot. Traffic from the airport was grim and it had taken him an extra two hours to manoeuvre his way past the accidents and road construction on the I-95. *Next time I'll use the Thruway – worth the $8.25.*

He spent the next two hours going through messages, checking in with his associate, Jim Kwan, who handled any client issues that couldn't wait for Grant personally, and bringing his personal finances and reports up to date.

"Jimmy, I'm going to drive down to Hallandale to see Kevin," Grant said as he closed and locked the file cabinet in his office. "Call me if anything comes up that needs my attention."

Grant decided to listen to music en route and not do much thinking, at least not for a while. Between the meeting in Boston, Larry finding his mother and Grant's own personal relationship with Jennie, the past three weeks had been pretty dramatic.

God is she hot! Smart, confident – she has everything. But it's not for me. And I don't know why. Just as well that she got the message last night. I can't take any more soap opera scenes. Of course nothing can ever top Lisa's bombshell.

Then his cellphone rang and Grant turned on his Bluetooth.

"Hi, Dad. I wouldn't call you in the car if it wasn't important," said Sam. "I have some stuff to tell you."

"Sam, not to worry buddy," answered Grant as he smiled. "What's up?"

"Well, you know that project on blood libel that Rhonda and I have been working on and that I told you about?" Sam asked.

"I remember you mentioning something about it," answered Grant.

"Well, here is what we now know, checked and doubled-checked. In 1928 there was a blood libel in Massena, NY."

Oh, oh, thought Grant.

"Anyway, a little girl went missing just after Rosh Hashanah and the townspeople went out to look for her. There was a café owned by a Greek immigrant named Albert Comnas who told the searchers that it must have been the Jews who did it. He said that in Europe the Jews needed the blood of Christians for their holidays and Yom Kippur was two days away. His hatred of Jews was a part of Greek orthodoxy that dates back over a thousand years. And as a result of his hate-mongering, a mob killed at least one old Jewish man, and there were two other guys found dead next to him just before the little girl was found safe and sound."

"Wow, what good research you and Rhonda have done," said Grant. "I'll bet you guys get a great mark."

"That's not why I am calling you Dad," Sam said in a cold voice, "a little more patience please."

Again Grant smiled.

"The Jewish man that was murdered that night was named Latchman – a name I've heard around us for a long time. I thought you would want to know."

Fuck, fuck! How does he know about Latchman?

"How do you know that I would be interested in anyone named Latchman?" asked Grant, knowing that it was a stupid question.

"Come on Dad!" Sam answered very forcefully. "A man named Latchman is associated with Uncle Peter. I've told you, in so many ways, about the internet and accessibility of information. Don't you think that I've looked on all the sites about Bubbie Rebecca and the DeLucas and Uncle Johnny? I've even looked you up. And so have my friends. That's just the way it is."

Guilty delusions, thought Grant. *We all suffered from guilty delusions. Lisa and I have worried for ten years about telling Sam about his heritage – something he already knows, at least in part.*

"Sam, you are so right, and I have been so wrong," said Grant. "Thanks for the information, which is definitely important to me right now. And congratulate Rhonda for me as well. You have done an outstanding research job, and I am so proud of you."

When Grant pulled into the driveway he'd already decided not to say anything to Lisa about his conversation with Sam until after the bar mitzvah. Both of them had obviously been living in la la land. He wanted to be with her when she realized how much Sam actually knew about his background and the people who were a part of his world. She was going to be very upset.

As he got out of his car, just inside the entrance, he heard Kevin calling him.

He turned and was surprised to see him walking hand in hand with Lisa. They were both laughing and Grant smiled as he noticed how much Kevin towered over her.

"Daddy, look who came to see me! It's Mommy Lisa!"

Lisa's face was lit up and her dimples were in full bloom as she smiled back at him.

They spent the next hour looking at Kevin's artwork, listening to his iPod and his own recordings and listening to him talk about all his adventures. Then they met with the staff and, as expected, all reports were good, Kevin was very well adjusted. He had occasional temper tantrums if he was teased by any of the other residents, but they were over quickly and forgotten.

Before Grant and Lisa left, they had their usual three-way bear hugs and did a little rock and sway that Kevin enjoyed.

"How did you get here?" asked Grant as he and Lisa started walking down the driveway.

"I got dropped off," she answered. "I was going to take the Greyhound back to Pte. St. Lucie, and then a taxi to the houseboat.

"But now that you've shown up," she continued, an ever widening Cheshire cat-like grin filling her face, "I hope that you'll let me hitchhike a ride back with you. Of course I'll be happy to pay for my share of the gas, if you insist."

It was almost five o'clock when they reached Pte. St. Lucie. It had been a very quiet ride as they were both happy to just listen to the music on the radio.

"Stop at the Publix just over there," said Lisa. "I'll pick up a couple of steaks and cook us dinner."

"Oh, how quaint," said Grant. "Are you sure? I'd be happy to go out for dinner. We can share the cost – equality and all that jazz."

"Oh, you are a smart-ass, or so you think," laughed Lisa. "Just pull over, and you'd better wait for me."

Cooking dinner had been a joint venture and now they were sipping on wine and continuing their barbs at one another. Some of it was just old-fashioned flirting, but mostly it was to avoid talking about the last few weeks and where that road was going to lead all of them.

"I know that we're avoiding the subjects that we should be discussing," Lisa finally said. "But I don't want to talk about it. I just want to sit here and enjoy the wonderful ocean breezes, the quiet, and, I do admit it, your company.

"Do you have a problem with that?" she asked him with a grin.

"Lisa, you really are too much," answered Grant returning her smile. "Come on out onto the deck. Bring your wine."

So there it was; a perfect scenario for any romantic love story. A full moon, ocean breezes, a gently swaying houseboat with a wide deck and two very attractive people standing next to each other. They shared a son and had maintained an open and affectionate relationship for many years as they each pretended that their drunken one night stand, which turned out to be not all that drunken, at least for Lisa, was the only intimacy between them. Now, at this moment and without any preamble or words spoken, they put down their wine glasses, wrapped their arms around each other and kissed.

Oh I still remember how he kissed me. This is better, much better, thought Lisa. She moved herself as close to him as she could.

Oh God, thought Grant. *She is so fucking delicious – what am I doing? What is going on here?*

Grant's hands slipped up under the back of Lisa's T-shirt and unhooked her bra. Her nipples were hard when he eased his palms across her breasts.

"You know, you are the best kisser," she whispered as she started moving her hips and pressing herself against Grant's erection. "I wonder how I could possibly know that. I seem to remember something. Have we met somewhere before?"

Grant threw back his head laughing. "Okay Lisa," he murmured as he leaned down to bury his head in her throat. "We're going inside, I am going to take off all your clothes and kiss you everywhere and then, who knows?"

"Oh, I already know," answered Lisa as she grabbed his buttocks and pulled him towards her. "And I can't wait."

CHAPTER TWENTY-ONE

Buffalo, New York.

Johnny Brattini was drinking a scotch on the rocks as he sat in the VIP suite waiting for his guests to arrive. This hotel was one of those fronted by a legitimate conglomerate, but it was actually owned by the Salerno crime family…and Brattini. It had been two days since Johnny returned from Boston – from the great day of revelations, as he liked to call it. Most of what he heard he already knew, though the details were somewhat disconcerting. And the sound of his father's voice as he spoke about Elizabeth's mother – that was too much for him. Johnny found himself wishing he had been a fly on the wall when Rebecca shot DeSalle. *If I had known then that he had also killed my father, I would have had his death spread over a much longer time frame. A bullet was too good for him.*

There was a loud knock at the door, and Johnny got up as one of his men opened it.

"Good to see you," said Yuri Latchman as he walked in and over to shake Johnny's hand. "How's your family?"

"Everyone's well," answered Johnny. "Thanks for asking. Do you want a drink?"

"Vodka ," answered Latchman as he sat down on the couch. He was wearing his usual attire: a black turtleneck jersey that showed off his muscular build. Yuri had huge muscles on his arms and a wide chest. He had begun shaving his head so that his face looked like a caricature of a Halloween mask.

Johnny was watching him and resisting a diabolical urge to tell him that it wasn't DeLuca who had killed his uncle Boris and taken what was left of his money, but him.

What Johnny didn't know was that Latchman was aware of the details of his uncle's murder – having been told by a third party in this triage, who believed that Brattini would soon have to be eliminated.

Latchman was a borderline nutcase. In 1928, his grandfather, who had been working as a gardener in Massena, NY, was murdered during a blood libel. He assumed that it was a few guys from the Mohawk tribe who had done it but there was no evidence, just rumours.

In 1976, Yuri's father, Vladimir, was haunted by a dream in which his father was calling to him. So he left his wife and baby son in the care of his brother, Boris, who gave him enough money to smuggle himself from Russia to the United States via Israel and the Refusenik sham. He eventually got to Massena where there were still some elderly Jews living just outside the town. They remembered the blood libel and took him to the Jewish cemetery and a communal plot of three unmarked graves, one of which belonged to his father. Vladimir said *Kaddish* and then swore over the graves that he would seek vengeance. Before he disappeared, never to be heard from again, he sent a hate letter in Yiddish to his toddler son, who first read it at the age of six:

> *You must exact revenge on this town and the Indians. Until you do, there will be no peace for my Tata and your Zayda. Show no mercy. Those goyim showed none to him. Always remember that they will kill us if we don't kill them first.*

Yuri always carried the note with him, sealed in plastic.

The buzzer sounded on the telephone. "Let him in," said Johnny as he got up and walked over to the door to open it.

"Hello Johnny, hello Yuri," said Howard Ramsay as he entered the room. "It's nice to finally be together in the same space. I assume the place is clean."

Johnny didn't bother answering, he just gave him a sneer.

Howard Ramsay was sixty-five years old. His white hair was sparse and his skin was a motley gray. He was very thin and very short, no more than five foot six. As Johnny looked at him, he tried not to burst out laughing. The video of Ramsay and the dog that Teasdale had given him kept planting itself in the front part of his brain. But Ramsay was probably the most powerful bureaucrat in Canada; something he had earned by using his position as the former Chief Judge on the Court of Appeal as his launching pad. As well there was his thirty plus years relationship with powerful politicians.

Johnny was always amazed at just how petty some of the rationale was to justify murder. He never rationalized anything. Business was business and he did whatever had to be done to get the deal finished.

Some people had *shticks* – a word often used by Lisa when they saw each other at family events, a word he now adopted as his own. Success in life didn't make the *shticks* go away, they were always there.

"Okay gentlemen," said Johnny pointing to the two chairs opposite the couch on which he was sitting. "The last two months of fuck-ups are now over. Who screwed up? What are your plans to fix it? I'm missing three million dollars in diamonds in what was supposed to be ordinary milk runs. And Yuri, what is this fucking fixation of yours with the border crossing between Cornwall and Massena? Start talking."

Latchman spoke first. "I'm planning to take over DeLuca Industries, legally." He ignored the smirk on Brattini's face.

"DeLuca's last two payments to Sierra Leone for the diamonds have been diverted to one of my offshore companies. He is now in arrears, though he doesn't know it yet.

"But I didn't expect those two shipments to get fucked up the way they did," he continued. "The runners thought they were moving money and drugs. It was the first time we were using Indians on this kind of a run and we wanted to see how they handled it. The explosion in Cornwall was totally unexpected. Some fucking cops were following them and, for some reason, blew up the van. And of course, they took the stones. I still don't know how they knew about that run."

You pig Russian, thought Ramsay. *How do you think they knew?*

"I put the diamonds in because Peter DeLuca was expecting his shipment from Sierra Leone via Kiev," Latchman went on. "And I didn't want him to get suspicious too soon. But those diamonds actually came from Israel as part of my preparation for transferring the P&M Trust money back to us. It was a test run for some of those Israeli exporters – that's what they like to call themselves. And of course, Howard was a part of it in order to test his Israeli operation."

That hooks you in, you dumb goy, thought Latchman. *Think I'm going to take the heat alone? No way, you prick.*

"And the second shipment in Juárez?" asked Johnny.

"Really it's the same story," answered Yuri. "But because it was on the Rio Grande, these guys were told to check out the crossing, specifically the distance between the two shores. For some reason they stopped at some shack and butchered the people living there. So that's probably the reason the Feds nailed them."

Ha, you really are a fucking idiot, thought Ramsay as he kept his eyes glued on Latchman.

"Do you know what information the Indians spit out?" asked Johnny.

"Nothing, as far as I know," answered Latchman. "But of course, the Feds got the diamonds."

Well, it looks like Larry's group really covered their asses, thought Johnny. *That's good for us, at least for now.*

"Was there anything else in those shipments?" asked Johnny, "anything that could possibly point a finger at us?"

"Not as far as I know," answered Yuri.

Not as far as I know, mimicked Ramsay in his head as he tried to keep a sneer off his face. *Asshole Jew!*

"I know that the Sierra Leone crowd isn't happy," said Johnny. "I got a message from them yesterday. Listen, we sure don't want them arriving here to sniff around.

"And I don't understand how you could have diverted DeLuca's money transfers to them," Johnny went on. "His people are very quick on the draw."

"Ha, they aren't that quick on the draw when it comes to my people," Latchman said with a smirk. "That fucking idiot Brattuso hasn't got a clue about what's going on right under his nose. Some genius he is. It turns out his right hand, Silvana, is an undercover Jew. Her mother is still living in Minsk, and I promised Silvana that if she was helpful, really helpful, I would bring her mother over here. Of course, I also promised her that I wouldn't tell anyone that she's Jewish. And she loves giving blow jobs. Naturally, I'm happy to accommodate her."

Ramsay made no attempt to hide his snickers. Latchman turned and glared at him.

Johnny needed a few seconds to restrain himself before continuing.

"Well, despite what you're saying Yuri, I still find it hard to believe that DeLuca and Brattuso are so clueless," he said. "But hey, it's your neck.

"Okay, now what is this crap about Massena, NY and Cornwall, Ontario?" asked Johnny. "There are any number of crossings between the US and Canada that the aboriginals can use, especially in Québec. Why are you so ratcheted up on this one?"

"I have a score to settle," said Latchman. "When this is done I intend to leave a present in the town, along with some dead Redskins."

"Well, you'd better make sure you cover your tracks better than you have so far," said Johnny. "My business associates can't afford to have any more problems with this operation. You sure wouldn't want them to get pissed off, would you Yuri?"

Latchman didn't answer. He just got up and walked over to the bar to get himself another drink.

Johnny then turned to Ramsay.

"Okay, Howard," he said. "You were supposed to make arrangements for a money transfer from Israel. You told me that you had the contacts to do it without anyone knowing about it."

"It's already in the works," answered Ramsay. "I have been working on it for a long time via the bureaucratic network – love that network – one back rub in exchange for another."

Ramsay laughed at what he obviously thought was a funny line. When no one else responded, he continued. "It is going to come via diplomatic courier. Rebecca Sherman's name was on that original fund that was used to buy the bonds. The cash value is now ten million dollars. It will be in the form of a Government of Israel money order made out to the estate of Rebecca Sherman. That dyke daughter of hers will receive it, and then sign it over."

"What, are you fucking crazy?" yelled Johnny with a sneer on his face to cover his rage at Ramsay's reference to Lisa. "She's never going to do that. And with Teasdale hanging all around and over her – what fairy tales are you telling yourself?"

"Ah, but you see, I've worked it all out," answered Ramsay with a smirk. "We are going to use those Indians and a brilliant strategy I have devised to get it all done. Money and retribution – all in one day and in one place – once and for all. Latchman will be satisfied and so will I."

"Of course, we can't do any of this without your organization," Ramsay continued as he smiled at Brattini, "especially when we bring in the Sicilians. So I think it's time to tell you about the plans that Yuri and I have worked out over the last few months – plans that are now ready to go."

"Yes, I agree," said Latchman. "It's time."

Outside the hotel sat a surveillance van disguised as a New York Power Authority repair truck. Johnny Brattini allowed members of Larry Lyon's team to wire his suite before he and his guests arrived. Two surveillance specialists surveyed the suite and situated a couch and two chairs to form an obvious place for Johnny to hold his meeting. On the wall behind the two chairs was a large painting. A long-range audio transmitter was installed on the top of the frame, above eye level and out of sight to anyone inside the suite. The audio feed transmitted to a central hub in the van outside. From there, anyone with a wireless connection, access to the FBI database and the access code set up for the feed could hear the conversation in real time.

In Washington, Bob Lantinos and Jennifer White were gathered around a conference table at FBI headquarters, listening to the feed from the large monitor mounted on the meeting room wall. Larry Lyons was listening alone in Toronto from his laptop, as were Grant Teasdale and Lisa Sherman in Florida. Grant had insisted that he listen to the feed alone, but Lisa was adamant and Grant knew that she would need to know everything at some point anyway.

Ramsay spoke first. "On Monday, June 25, Teasdale, Lisa and their kid will be in Toronto.

"The Mayor, Carl Ashton, who is one of mine by the way, has arranged to close one of the municipal golf courses to the public in order to host a father and son invitational tournament with proceeds going to charity. We have even arranged for special golf hats," giggled Ramsay.

"Ashton called Teasdale last month to personally invite him to participate. He was quite enthusiastic because he expected to be in town that weekend anyway. Apparently Jews have a memorial or something before any big event – in this case the kid's bar mitzvah – and they visit the graves of their dead relatives to invite them. Sounds like crap to me. Hey, Yuri, do you ever do that?"

"Not lately," was Latchman's reply, even though he knew all about it, causing him to have an unexpected twinge in his gut.

"But Teasdale isn't Jewish so why will he there?" asked Johnny.

"Teasdale told Ashton that he was planning to join Lisa and Sam at the gravesite of that bitch Rebecca and other relatives on the Sunday before the tournament," answered Ramsay. "Some sort of crap about prayer and respect being shown. He said that he would have no problem arranging to have everyone stay for an extra day especially since it would give him and Sam an opportunity to play competitive golf as a team – and he was quite enthusiastic about that – so he happily accepted Ashton's invite."

Holy fuck, what a brilliant set up, thought Grant as he took Lisa's hand. She looked a bit stressed and gave his hand a squeeze.

THE THIRD HOLE

"Once they are on the course, Latchman's Indians get their chance to shine," laughed Ramsay as he continued talking. "First the mother and then the kid will be nabbed and then she will have five minutes to sign. One of Latchman's Jews has already witnessed the document."

"He is an Israeli," snapped Latchman. "There is a big difference."

"Come on Yuri, a Jew is a Jew, no matter what country they come from."

"Okay guys," said Johnny. "You have made this story sound like a one, two, three operation, but there will be so many people around and so many security people because of the VIP's who usually play in these events. Explain to me how this can possibly work out? And how can one person close a whole golf course?"

"Well, you don't know how Canadian municipalities work," answered Ramsay with a smirk. "The Mayor can do anything he wants when it comes to a municipal golf course, which is what the Toronto Valley Golf Course is. So all he has to do is get several of his city councillors to back him and that's it – the course will be closed. Of course it's on a Monday, their slowest day, and the city will be getting the money lost on the day's revenues…if Ashton decides to share it with them."

Johnny asked Latchman what role the select Mohawk men had to play in all this.

"Ah," answered Latchman. "That's where those practice diamond runs come in handy. The two fucked-up raids were part of ten runs done over the last two years. There are seven men left from the original group of fourteen; five others were killed by the feds and two went missing in Juárez. One of those left is a pilot and the others are the aboriginal versions of the Green Berets."

"Okay, so explain to me what the plan is in a simple way that I can understand," said Johnny. "I admit that the whole scenario strikes me as insane…but I know that you're not insane Yuri."

"No, I'm not insane," said Latchman. "I'm just anxious to get this over with so I can piss on DeLuca's grave and then take over the company. After that, I go back to Kiev for a visit – and to see how much gratitude the Russian president shows to me."

"Have you had a dry run?" asked Johnny. "I mean, tell me how you can be so sure that these guys will know what you want from them, especially since they probably haven't been able to get a good layout of the site."

"Actually, they have," Ramsay answered. "The guys who will be coming in to grab the kid and his mother have been going over the 3rd hole for the last two weeks, arriving at the course every morning at five o'clock. There's enough light and they have special goggles to help get the layout burned into their brains before the first golfers start arriving to tee off at six fifteen in the morning. The security guards belong to the city and they have been paid off. Or we can only hope that Ashton has paid them off.

"Once the regular golfers do arrive, the Indians take off. They're staying at a hotel in the downtown area of the city; an area that is close to the agencies that serve the Native population so they fit right in and are not noticed."

"And what do you think that Teasdale is going to be doing when you snatch his kid?" asked Brattini, his face blank and his voice sounding somewhat amused. "The first sound of guns or yelling or anything and the whole course comes alive – 911 calls from surrounding homes, cops showing up everywhere, even the other golfers who will start crossing over the fairway to see what's going on."

"Yes, we have thought about that," answered Ramsay. "Thank the Lord for silencers...and other good stuff. Teasdale's group is booked last, they're the final group. Everyone else will be well ahead of them. And just to make sure, we have also put a very slow foursome in front of them. And of course, I will be playing in Teasdale's group."

"Hey! When did you have a son?" Latchman sneered. "I thought you could only get it up with dogs."

Ramsay actually jumped out of his chair and started towards Latchman.

"Cut it out!" snapped Johnny as he got up and stood between the two men. "Sit back down both of you. You know that Rebecca had a copy of that tape and no doubt showed it around. I'll bet Peter has seen it too.

"Howard, you didn't really answer my question about snatching the kid," continued Johnny. "So I think this is just an unrealistic dream you're having. You know, get rid of anyone who knows anything about your past, then you're ready to go. But what about the video itself? Any clue on where it is?"

"I know that cunt gave it to Teasdale," answered Howard as he sat back down. "Watching one of my Indians use a knife on his kid will no doubt persuade him to start singing."

Lisa couldn't help but let out a gasp as she looked at Grant. He nodded at her and whispered "sh, sh."

"Well is that it?" said Johnny. "I'm going to be in Cleveland with my family that weekend. I'm almost tempted to cancel my trip so I can see first-hand if this exercise of yours is going to work.

"But I doubt that it is," he continued. "Sounds like a cowboys and Indians old-time TV show. How are all those Indians going to get into a golf course without causing a stir?"

"Faith, my dear Mr. Brattini," answered Ramsay. "You have to have faith."

"Well, I would rather have the facts," said Johnny, "since it is my money that's paying for this – and my associates who will have to share the costs if you guys fuck it up."

"I can't give you any more facts," answered Ramsay. "My guys have been working with Latchman's Indians for some time now, and they want it all kept between them. Even I don't have all the details.

"But they know that they won't get paid if the job isn't done," he went on, "and done right. So go on your trip John, enjoy yourself, and make sure you're able to get back in time for all the funerals."

Ramsay knows, thought Grant, *because he isn't telling any more than he has to. He obviously doesn't trust Johnny.*

"Yuri, what about you in all this?" asked Johnny. "These are the guys that you trained – nice that you have just turned them all over to Howard."

"Actually, there will only be five of them up in Toronto," answered Latchman. "They're all who are needed as long as things go according to plan. I am meeting the other two and a hardwired SUV in Massena, NY, on that Monday. I have a gift for the townspeople and I want to be close by when they get it."

When the two men had left, Johnny put his legs on the coffee table, sat back on the couch, closed his eyes and thought again of Lisa. Even though she had been in a relationship with Isobel for years, it was now over. His gut had always told him that she was a man's woman and that her relationship with Isobel was an anomaly. Maybe Lisa just went both ways – something he didn't understand and had no desire to learn more about. But since his feelings were personal and this was business, he pushed Lisa out of his head.

Johnny knew that nothing would change the quid pro quo that was a part of his world. Perhaps the attacks would become more subtle, perhaps the methodology less crude, but at the end of the day, the same principle was there: "You do, I do." Despite the myriad of words written about the business he and Peter were in, some things had not changed in one hundred years and never would – payback – and if the focus had become blurred over sixty years, too bad. There still had to be payback. Johnny intended to make sure that it was him, and those he cared about, who were standing at the end of the day – not Ramsay and not Latchman.

Johnny picked up one of his disposable cellphones. He kept a large supply of them in his house, his office, and with him wherever he went.

"Hello, Peter."

"Hey, John," answered Peter. "Angela and the girls are at a bridal shower or something so you and I can gossip all we want."

Johnny smiled at Peter's attempt at lightness. He knew, as they all knew, that underneath the surface they had a crisis of potentially devastating proportions. They also knew that they would have to work together to fix it.

"I'm going to be at Worcester Airport in an hour to pick you up," Johnny said. "Have your driver wait with you on the tarmac until the plane doors open and then he can leave. Tell my sister the truth – that we are both flying down to Florida to have a meeting with Grant

Teasdale. I expect this to be a twelve hour exercise from start to finish."

"Did you get everything we need?" asked Peter.

"I got it."

CHAPTER TWENTY-TWO

Grant was asleep on his back with Lisa's leg and arm draped across him when his cellphone started vibrating and honking. She heard it first and poked him awake. It was two o'clock in the morning. He put his arm around her while he checked the caller ID.

"Hi Johnny," he said. Lisa sat upright and the colour left her face. She made no attempt to cover herself.

"My plane will be landing at Witham Field in an hour," said Johnny. "That's about half an hour away from you. Peter is with me and I told him what you've already heard. We're going to have a meeting on board."

"Okay," said Grant. "I'll be there."

Lisa didn't move when Grant clicked off the cellphone. Her big brown eyes were glued on his as he put his hands on her waist and pulled her next to him. He turned so that they were both lying on their sides, facing each other.

"If you don't agree to marry me, sooner rather than later, I will not have sex with you ever again."

It took Lisa a few seconds to register what he had said before she burst out laughing. Grant then pulled her closer and put his arms around her. She couldn't resist the urge to push her body against his very erect penis.

"Well, are you prepared to convert?" she asked as her hands started gently rubbing his buttocks.

"Well, since the circumcision part isn't an issue, thank goodness," he answered in a whisper as he pulled her closer so that he could kiss her, "it would be my honour."

"Oh Grant, you can be such a jerk," she whispered in his ear as her hand moved to the front of his body. "Why would I ever want you to be anything other than what you are? And despite pretending otherwise, I know that your Catholicism is important to you. I was just teasing you."

They hugged for another minute or two in silence.

"Okay, time to go," said Grant as he sat up abruptly. "I have to leave here in less than half an hour to meet Peter and Johnny at Witham."

"I'm going with you," said Lisa as she also got up and out of the bed. "It really would be a waste of your time to try and stop me. It's my life at risk and that of our son. I am not prepared to sit by the fire waiting to hear what strategy and decisions are being made without my input."

"I'm not surprised," said Grant as he pulled on his pants, "and I'm not going to try to stop you. And you know what else? I agree with you. But I guarantee you that both Peter and Johnny will have a hissy fit. Women don't fit into their operations.

"They will be concerned that you won't be able to handle whatever is bound to fall in our faces," he continued, "or that you might talk too much, or that you might interfere in their plans, which I'm sure they have no intention of sharing with you."

"That's fine," said Lisa as she pulled a sweatshirt over her jeans. "At least I'll have an opportunity to put in my two cents' worth and maybe I'll even be able to help."

"Assuming they allow you to be present during the meeting, my suggestion is that the less you say, the better it will be," said Grant. "I'll answer anything you don't understand right there. Later, when we are alone, you can speak to any of your suspicions, of which I guarantee there will be many."

"Okay," said Lisa. She looked at Grant and smiled as her eyes filled with tears. "It means so much to me being able to count on you and know that you're always there. Oh, by the way, I do love you. I think I always have."

When Grant and Lisa pulled onto the tarmac their car was blocked by two black SUV's. A flashlight scanned their faces before they were allowed to continue driving to the plane, parked at the western end of the runway. When their car was about fifty yards away, Lenny Brattuso appeared out of nowhere, or so it seemed. Behind him were two other burly-looking types.

"Hi Lisa," said Lenny when they got out of the car. "Peter didn't mention that you would be here."

"That's because he didn't know," she said. "But I am here, and I intend to stay."

Lenny smiled as he turned to use his cell. There was a very brief exchange and then he turned back and said with a smile, "alright, the two bosses say okay."

"Two bosses?" asked Lisa. "Who are the two bosses?"

"Not to worry Lisa," said Grant. Then he extended his hand to Lenny.

"Good to see you again Inspector," said Lenny. "And please don't have any concerns about security. We are all around the perimeter. Johnny's guys are also everywhere."

"I have no concerns," Grant said as he took Lisa's arm and started towards the plane's stairs. Then he stopped and turned back to Lenny.

"I met your father many years ago when I had a meeting with Santino," he said smiling. "Vinnie was a loyal and dependable man and I enjoyed our brief conversation, especially his jokes about the mangia-cakes."

Lenny smiled and nodded his head.

The interior of Johnny's plane was very impressive. It was a Cessna Citation, Longitude; it could go four thousand miles and the interior had a flat area of thirty-one feet. Lots of stand-up space and the perks were spectacular: touch-screen control on everything – lighting, window shades, temperature, digital audio and video and a real time map. Furnishings were beige leather swivel seats and a large desk. There was also a table that could seat eight and when it wasn't needed, it was folded into a small side table on which sat a vase full of fresh roses. The galley was nicer than some homes Lisa had seen and the bathroom was all glass. The bedroom door was closed but Lisa was sure it would also be spectacular.

Once inside, Lisa hugged both Peter and Johnny before she raised her hands.

"Think of me as Mrs. Moses standing at the edge of the Red Sea," she said. "Just where you would pass over the water to the Promised Land. I will pass on to you the words received from the Mount."

Despite himself, Johnny started to laugh. Peter just smiled, though it looked rather weak.

"I am ready to listen," Lisa began. "But there will be no decisions taken that involve me or Sam without my input. I know that I don't know everything, but I also don't have any hang-ups when it comes to what you guys do, though I prefer not to know the details. I suppose that could be interpreted as denial and maybe it is. We have been together as family for over twelve years," Lisa continued. "I know Sam means a lot to all of you…and I know that I do as well. Rest assured that wherever this road leads, I will be ready to do whatever it takes to protect my son. You can count on me."

Grant turned and looked at her in silence. *Oh, you are your mother's daughter. No panic, no hysteria, just the facts. You will do what you have to do, and why do I absolutely know that there will be no hesitations and no second guesses.*

Johnny just stood quietly as well, a sad smile on his face. Then he took charge.

"Okay, everyone, sit down," he said. "The steward will bring in some fruit, juices, some toasted bagels and some cheeses, tea and coffee. Then all the staff on this plane, including the pilot will deplane so we can be alone. I've had the plane swept to insure there are no hidden ears, either directly or from outside the aircraft. However, I still want you to think about how you say whatever it is you want to say. Keep the front page of the newspapers in your mind as the yardstick."

"Geez Johnny," said Lisa laughing. "When did you get to be so exciting? How could I have missed it all these years? This is just like a James Bond movie. I love it."

"Very funny Lisa," snapped Johnny. "This isn't a joke...so smarten up!"

Grant noticed an intimacy between Johnny and Lisa that their banter revealed. No problem for him, it was more curiosity than anything else.

When everyone was seated around the table, Johnny placed one of the cellphones on it. It was hooked into a microphone. He clicked a button.

"Larry," he said, "we're all here including an additional guest – Lisa."

"Oh, come on Lisa," Larry moaned over the speaker. "Why? You're adding to your risk."

Grant put out his arm to stop Lisa from speaking.

"Hey bro," he said. "There's no point in trying to keep her away. She knows her and Sam are targets. So let's not spend any time on a wasted exercise. We know what has to be done and she's on my team. Johnny and Peter will have no interference."

"I, too, am not happy with your presence here Lisa," said Peter, "but after all these years, I know that trying to change your mind is more aggravating than challenging. So I'll rely on Grant to keep you in line."

"Now to business," Johnny said. "How was the stuff that I got for you a few hours ago Larry? PC, I hope."

"Perfect," answered Larry. "I'm off to Washington as soon as this call is over. They were just as pleased as I was. Now I intend to make sure all the loose ends are cut off before the next move."

"Good. I thought there might be some kind of bizarre justice in letting those two pigs hang themselves with their own words," said Johnny. "Okay, Peter and I have discussed some strategy on the way down here," Johnny said. "What we are going to do now is agree on how much Lisa and Sam are needed."

Lisa sat quietly and just looked at Grant.

"Well, you had better give me the different scenarios and what plans you have in mind," said Grant, "and then I will let you know how Lisa and Sam could be involved…if at all."

"I don't want to hear any of the details," said Larry. "I can't know anything about it yet. Just remember to cover your specific asses. As I told you in Boston, whatever you do is up to you. You can do your thing and we'll do what we have to do from here. Grant and I will discuss my team's involvement once he knows your strategy and how much we need to know. So that is it for me. I'll be back in Toronto in a couple of days. Good luck!"

Larry disconnected the speaker phone from his end and everyone was quiet for a few minutes. Then Johnny spoke.

"As far as you are concerned Lisa, we believe that it is a waste of time to try and fool anyone, especially the bad guys we are facing. In today's world of high-tech cyber-hacking, digital cameras and voice identity tools, there is no point in even thinking about using stand-ins, no matter how close they look to the key players."

"And who are the key players?" asked Lisa before Grant could stop her.

"You…and Sam," answered Peter. "Johnny and I have spent the last few hours trying to come up with something, anything, to avoid your direct involvement. So far we've come up with nothing. But no matter what, this time they will not get away. And there will be no mercy shown," he said more to himself than anyone else.

Grant stood up and started to walk around the small space in the plane's lounge.

"For the first time in a very long time, I believe that this planned attack will be the last," Grant said, "one way or another. And I intend to make sure that it is another. Ramsay is obviously not telling it all," he continued. "He either suspects Johnny of some double-cross or he and Latchman are planning to finish you both off as well. I vote that they are planning to finish you both off.

"The good part for us is that Latchman is a borderline psychotic," Grant went on, "or maybe not so borderline. He might make a mistake. Rebecca once told me that she thought he must have known that it was Johnny who killed his Uncle Boris, not Santino. If that's true, then we have to assume we are being placated and are only being told a part of their plan, not all of it."

Then Peter stood up and followed Grant on his pacing around the plane's lounge.

"I have a meeting in two days with Latchman in my office," said Peter. "I'll see what I can find out and I'll let you know."

No one looked at or spoke to Lisa. Then she stood up and started to walk around the lounge.

"I guess you are all waiting to hear from me," she said as she tried a tentative smile. "My first question is – hard to even say it out loud, but I need to understand – why don't they just kill all of us and be done with it?"

"It's not that simple," answered Peter. "That only works in the movies. There are business associations and personal ties. For each person that might be eliminated, there would be many others wanting to know why and wouldn't stop until they got the answer. We are not an isolated group – we have our hands in so many places.

"Latchman knows that for sure," Peter went on. "And so does Ramsay. So what good would it be to eliminate their enemies but never be done with the friends of their enemies? This has been the weakness and, on occasion, the strength of our families over these past fifty years.

"So whatever plan they think they have," Peter continued, "will have to be done cleanly and without any questions. I would guess some sort of set-up accident, similar to the one that killed Boris Latchman so many years ago. But this doesn't look like it can be made to look like any accident. So I admit that we're not sure, and that's causing me some stress."

"Okay," said Lisa. "I get that, I really do. But what is incredible is that I'm standing here calmly talking to you about what the best way to murder me is. Will I ever be the same after this experience?"

"Yes, you will," Johnny answered as he walked over and put his arm around her shoulder. "And I agree – it is incredible. You're being so brave about it. But don't forget that we are all in this together."

Lisa sighed. "Now I have another question. What kind of computer is this PC that everyone is talking about? Does it mean personal computer?"

All three men burst out laughing. "Let me," said Grant as he waved off Peter and Johnny.

"It means 'probable cause' Lisa," answered Grant. "Because of the information you have heard and some that you haven't heard, INSETs and the FBI will be able to get subpoenas and court orders for wire taps to access their home and office internet and to surveillance both Ramsay and Latchman. In the case of Ramsay, it gives INSETs access to all his contacts and who he's been dealing with around the globe. There are a lot of ramifications, especially in finding out which bureaucrats in other countries are his allies.

"And with probable cause, the government agents can also access Latchman's contacts, his Russian associates here in North America and even his political friends in Russia and around the world.

"And the best part of all this is that any evidence obtained can be used in court!" Grant said with a big grin on his face. "To quote that famous TV ad: PC is priceless!"

"Well, that's interesting to know," said Lisa, her voice surprisingly calm. "And now I guess it's my turn to give you my take on what I have just heard and what I now believe has to be done.

"I want this to be over," she continued very forcefully even though her eyes started to fill up. "All the information discussed at our meeting in Boston is much clearer to me now. Sam and I will have to play out our roles because I want him to have a chance at life. There is no other way. The only caveat that I insist upon is that Sam sits down with his father and me in order to have an opportunity to ask any questions before he makes his own decision about participating. That means that he will have to be told what is going on and that his life is at risk."

Lisa looked over at Grant who remained silent. The she turned back to Johnny and continued. "After Sam has made his decision, I will look to you and to Peter to provide him with the best protection that's out there. It is my absolute belief that if we don't act now, and act with finality, it will remain a cloud and a threat over all of our lives forever, especially his…and he is only thirteen years old."

None of the men answered her right away. Then Peter DeLuca, who was already thinking about his upcoming meeting with Latchman, said, "Lisa, Sam will be protected. There's no chance of those pigs getting their hands on him."

Then Lisa walked over to Peter and hugged him. Johnny was next. And then Grant.

"Lisa, you are very special," whispered Grant.

For Johnny, it was another disappointment, though not unexpected. He loved Lisa as a buddy and as a secret 'wish it could happen but never would' lover. But he would use everything in his power and everything he owned to protect her and Sam as long as he lived.

When Grant and Lisa left the plane, it was close to six o'clock in the morning and the sun was on the rise behind some black clouds. Their car was sitting at the bottom of the plane's stairs and Lenny was standing next to the driver's door. For some reason, Lisa went over and hugged him before she and Grant got into the car and pulled away.

CHAPTER TWENTY-THREE

Washington, D.C.

Larry Lyons and Jennifer White had been sitting with Bob Lantinos having coffee in his office for almost half an hour before Jake Bartoli came bounding in accompanied by David Awasake, an undercover RCMP operative.

David Awasake's incredible skills had resulted in him earning the rank of Colonel, very unusual for an undercover. He also happened to be of aboriginal decent. David was a member of the Métis Nation, unique from First Nations in Canada as most Métis ancestors were of mixed white and aboriginal blood. He had been recommended by Inspector William Walker, the Superintendant of the RCMP, after the prime minister's executive assistant had made a call, a call recommended by the president.

"So far, we have the absolute best in this operation," Walker had said. "Let's make sure that the Canadian contingent is at the same level."

David Awasake had a similar background to Larry Lyons and Grant Teasdale. Abandoned in a Québec orphanage that "specialized" in aboriginal Canadians, David had been beaten regularly but had not been sexually assaulted as Larry and Grant had been. When he was eighteen he joined the RCMP and rose quickly in the ranks.

"I know what you are all asking yourselves right now," laughed Bartoli. "Why is this Canadian standing at my right arm? And what can this mean for Larry Lyons?"

Larry got up and went over to shake David's hand. "It's nice to finally meet you in person," said Larry. "Your excellent reputation precedes you. And oh yes, ignore Bartoli's attempts at humour. He really has a limited personality. I've never understood why Bob is so nice to him."

"Very funny," quipped Jake. "Anyhow, RCMP Superintendant Walker had no problem with my co-opting David to this operation. So here he is, and here we are. How about giving me an update, Bob?"

"Actually, Larry is the best one to fill you in," answered Lantinos. "And after that we can all knock it around. But before I let him do that, there is still one matter that has to be resolved Jake." Bartoli smiled and waited for Bob to speak.

"At the outset of this investigation," Lantinos said, "both the US and Canadian governments agreed to indemnify certain key players in exchange for their cooperation on any matters relating to themselves, their families or their businesses relevant to this operation only.

"On that clear understanding," he went on, very slowly, "information has now been gathered from those key players. Before that information can be shared with you and the other members of the team, we want a signed waiver by the Attorney General and the Minister of Justice corroborating their original verbal undertaking. We will also be deleting any material not specific to the matter under investigation from those documents."

"Just give me the bottom line, Bob," said Jake.

"No actual evidence will be handed over until the commitments given to get them are fulfilled," said Lantinos. "And I am in full agreement that those commitments are to be the originals."

"Bob, do we have PC?" asked Jake.

"You will," answered Bob, "as soon as the signed indemnity is in hand."

"So my word won't do it?" asked Jake, half laughing, half hoping. But he already knew the answer.

"Okay, never mind," he went on. "Luckily I figured that you would be in a mistrusting mood, even here, so I asked for the document yesterday when I got your first hint about the PC. I understand it will be here by four in the afternoon. So now, how about a short story on what is going down?" asked Jake. "I'm sure David is very interested."

All eyes turned to David who was still staring at Jennifer. She was standing by the far window leaning against its ledge.

Later that night, Larry got a call from Grant. "Have Lantinos send White and Awasake here, to Pte. St. Lucie, as soon as they can leave Washington," he said without any preamble. "This thing is going down in Toronto on the twenty-fifth of June so we need to act fast. Make sure they understand that when we get to Toronto their backup will be a private group; I'm sure Jennie knows who they work for."

"Okay," answered Larry. "Do you still want me to pick up Kevin on my way back?"

"Yes, for sure," answered Grant. "Lisa's tenant in the Tranby property has moved out so we are all going to stay there from June twenty-second until we go to Boston on June twenty-seventh."

"Who's 'we'?" asked Larry.

"Lisa, Elizabeth, Sam, Kevin and me. Actually, do me a favour and call Elizabeth. She's waiting for Lisa to come back before the two of them and Sam fly up to Toronto. Ask her to bring Sam as soon as she can. Lisa is staying with me until we are ready to join her. It's a slight change in logistics, so feel free to answer any of her questions. But I think she will know without asking.

"Oh yes, and tell her not to hire any cleaning people for the Tranby house," he went on. "I don't want anyone in there besides us, period. If necessary, I'll practice my soon-to-be domesticity."

"What?" Larry yelped. "Does that mean what I think it does?"

"I hope so," answered Grant as he turned in the bed and nuzzled Lisa's neck.

"And I think Jennifer and Awasake should also stay at Tranby. It's a big house."

"Okay, I'll put a twenty-four hour on it, starting June twenty-second."

"No, do it now," said Grant, his voice getting very tense. "I'm not sure what the final details are yet, but I want to make sure there are no surprise guests, connections, or cameras."

"Okay, I get it," said Larry. "It will all be in place before morning. The warrants have been executed, selectively at the moment, but later in full. Everything is in writing along with happy faces. Message for you to pass along is 'well done'.

"I'm going to fly down there sooner rather than later to pick up Kevin – probably day after tomorrow," Larry continued. "Make sure that you do all the clearance stuff with the Home. I don't feel like having an argument with some ding-dong bureaucrat. Kevin can stay with me and my mother until you guys arrive. I'll bring him over to Tranby when you are settled in."

"Thanks bro," said Grant, his voice softening. "You never let me down."

"Hey," he whispered in Lisa's ear as he put the telephone down. "You still haven't given me an official answer to my proposal."

"What proposal?" she asked as she stretched out on the bed and her hands began moving down his body to stroke his penis and the surrounding territory.

"Well, it wasn't an actual proposal," he answered as he turned onto his back so she could have unfettered access to his private parts. "It was an ultimatum. Remember? I said that if you didn't agree to marry me we would never have sex again."

"Oh," she giggled. "But what I'm doing right now isn't a 'we,' it's a 'you.'"

Grant grabbed her shoulders and flipped her onto her back. He put his lips on one of her nipples and sucked gently as he massaged the other one with his thumb and forefinger.

Lisa started to move and a moan escaped her lips.

Grant got up on his knees, opened her legs and lifted them around his back.

"This is a 'we,'" he said as he grabbed her buttocks and thrust himself into her wetness. "And now it's too late for me to stop," he moaned as he kissed her and let the spasms of ecstasy roll over them both.

CHAPTER TWENTY-FOUR

Jennifer White and David Awasake caught a flight from Washington to Orlando and then to Pte. St. Lucie. They arrived at midnight. They rented a car and drove to the houseboat. On the way they had a chance to chat and share personal information – not too personal, but enough to create a friendly working relationship.

Awasake was thirty-five years old. He was almost six feet tall, had long jet-black hair that he wore in a ponytail and his skin colour was olive. In other words, he looked exactly like the outdated white man's perception of an aboriginal and he knew it. David had a great sense of humour, especially about his looks. He was a man who loved the best. Off duty, he dressed only in Armani.

When David had studied the history of his ancestors in high school, he was surprised to learn that they were the offspring from unions between aboriginals and European settlers. The Métis people were also traders, merchants, politicians and translators. Unfortunately, their past conflicts in western Canada created a negative attitude towards them and they were driven away to the East. Most settled in Québec which is where David was born.

David was surprised at how jealous he was when he heard the story of Larry Lyons and his mother from Jennifer during their drive. It was a reminder that no matter how deep we think we push our pain or longing away, it is always sitting there waiting to pop out when we least expect it. Given the sad history of aboriginals' family services in

Canada, he knew that he would never learn about his family history, nor would anyone ever come looking for him. He appreciated that his early life could have been worse. He wasn't sexually abused by some creep priest, but the beatings he endured from other people, including some of the nuns in the orphanage where he was dumped, were a part of his psyche. He had never had any desire to have children of his own and decided that since he wasn't a psychiatrist, he wasn't going to worry about why.

Jennie chatted away about her background and her love of her work and that she, like David, had no desire to have any children. Given the diversity of their backgrounds, it was an interesting similarity. She was glad that no one other than Larry knew about her short fling with Grant Teasdale. Gossip was rampant in the policing world and it often amazed her how much personal information, especially about sexual activities, was known by so many.

So she was happy that she could maintain her professional detachment and not worry about any snarky remarks being made behind her back.

"I think this is the second day, or is it night, that I've been sleep free," said Lisa when David and Jennifer finally arrived at the houseboat and she welcomed them on board.

"Grant is just checking out something in the engine, or whatever the thing is called that controls the air circulation. I have fresh coffee, or tea or juice. Are you guys hungry? How about something to eat – cookies? Some fruit?"

"Thanks, I'd love an orange juice," answered Jennie as she dropped her bag on the floor and extended her hand. "And it's so nice to finally meet you in person. You have two great admirers in *The Brothers Karamazov*."

"Count me in too," laughed David as he took Lisa's hand, "as an admirer and also as a man desperate for a cold drink. Orange juice will be great."

When Grant joined them, Lisa didn't miss the mist in Jennie's eyes as she looked at him.

Forget it baby, thought Lisa. *He's mine.*

Lisa decided that she didn't need to be a part of the group – Grant would tell her whatever she needed to know. She was going to take a shower and then go to sleep.

"Excuse me everyone," she said after pouring the juice and putting a bowl of grapes on the table. "I'm dead, so if you don't mind I'm heading off to bed. See you in the morning." Then she walked over to Grant and kissed him gently on the lips.

"Yes, I will," she whispered. The smile and look in his eyes told her that he got her message.

They were sitting on the outside deck; the sky was lit up with the stars and the moon, and there were candles burning on the tables. Not the usual spot for this kind of police work but it was a nice change. Then the three of them started brainstorming possible strategies based on what little information they had.

Grant was feeling a bit uncomfortable about Jennie and Lisa together in such close quarters. He was relieved that the meeting earlier between the two of them had gone okay – certainly not the kind of scene he would expect in a movie, but then again, Lisa had no idea about his relationship with Jennie. So now here he was – working with one woman with whom he had experienced such passionate, uninhibited sex just one week ago, and then, yesterday, finally acknowledging his deep love for another woman – the mother of his son – a woman with whom he had spent the last twenty-four hours naked and aroused and finally, spent.

I suppose I could make a sick joke about my age and this being my last hurrah, thought Grant as he struggled to concentrate on the ongoing discussion. *But I think I won't do that and simply relish the moments. At some point, when this is over, I'll sit down with Jennie and talk it out.*

Jennifer looked over at Grant and took her own moment for self assessment. She knew it was over between them, really, before it had ever begun. She would move on, she always did. But this time she was feeling quite sad – sad for the emptiness that she knew would be a part of her life again and sad for her acceptance of it.

THE THIRD HOLE

Oh well. Now is not the time to dwell in self-pity. You know who you are – you know what you have always wanted – so far you've had it all – put him away. He's gone.

David spoke first. "I'm concerned because this kidnapping – murder plot sounds so amateurish and unrealistic," he said, "and the players involved are anything but that – Latchman in particular. That man is a butcher. We have reports from Kiev about the goon squad that he uses there as his reps. And I also don't think he's over endowed in the brain department.

"I agree with David," said Jennie. "This is still not sitting right with me either. My gut is twitching. We're missing something. Let's walk through the scenario of June twenty-fifth again.

David and Grant stretched out on their chairs and put their feet up on the table. It was two o'clock in the morning.

"A charity golf tournament...very expensive," began Jennifer. "There are eighty players. The golf course is just off a main road. It's set well back with huge maple trees and masses of bushes. It's also down in a valley. There's also a major highway overhead that runs east – west. Start time is three o'clock on every hole and Teasdale's group is expected to reach the 3rd hole at around four. The round is expected to end in four and a half hours so there will still be light.

"The clubhouse will be set up for a large reception before and after the matches," she went on. "There will be all kinds of staff and volunteers. The good news is that there's only one entrance and exit to the clubhouse." Grant and David said nothing.

"Okay, first thing," Jennie said as she got up and started pacing along the deck. "We must have the names of everyone who is supposed to be there. Grant, you get Latinos to create some kind of anonymous threat; one of the players who's coming to play is Senator Jack Simpson from New York, so use him as the excuse. That'll not only force the organizers to have a master list that has to be checked off, but also allows security from the US to be there as well. And tell him to assign me as the head of it. I'll do a check of the whole area early that morning. I'll need a specially equipped golf cart with a special key so only I can use it – never know who's waiting for a slip.

Okay, now I'm starting to feel a bit better," laughed Jennifer as she continued talking very fast. There was nothing like a formidable challenge to get all her parts working at their best.

"Grant, what about the other security men that Lantinos talked about?" she asked. "Who are they and how will I know them?"

"They won't be what we would usually call our security men," answered Grant with a wry smile on his face. "The men you will both be working with are part of the DeLuca and Brattini teams and will be wearing identifying hats. Their job is to take care of the perps. As we discussed in Washington, where they and you are concerned, this will be a case of 'see nothing, speak nothing'. Sam and Lisa are their primary focus. Ramsay and Latchman are the FBI and INSETs' focus.

"INSETs is also making two special golf hats for Sam and me that will be slipped into the box of hats that will be distributed to all the players. I'll know what to look for."

"Okay," Jennie piped in again. "Let's continue with our scenario. So everyone is now on the course – swinging long poles, riding in open carts, drinking beer and looking for lost balls or whatever you people do when you play that ridiculous game."

David and Grant smiled, but refrained from making any comments.

Jennie continued walking back and forth along the deck. "Grant, I still can't figure out how they can grab Lisa and Sam, neutralize you, get Lisa to sign the release and have nobody notice? Something's missing here and it's driving me crazy."

Silence. Then David turned to Grant and said, "so if your suspicion about Ramsay knowing more than he's letting on is correct, and I think it is, we've got to be...."

"FUCK! FUCK! FUCK!" screeched Jennie, stopping in her tracks. "I think I just figured it out! An explosion! It has to look like an accident! It'll have to happen somewhere on the course far away from the 3rd hole. It'll be the distraction needed so that everyone will start running towards it, giving them enough time to grab Grant and Sam. It'll also give them a good chance to escape with their hostages before anyone notices they're gone."

THE THIRD HOLE

Grant stood up. "Holy shit Jennie!" he said excitedly. "You're so right! That's the only way that it can work! I should have thought of that myself. I play that course with Larry almost every time I come up to Toronto. The 3rd hole is at the south end of the property, quite a distance from the bridge overpass which is at the northern boundary. There's been ongoing construction under that bridge right near the 18th hole for five years now. There are lots of trucks and workmen and equipment. And I'll bet the gas mains run right along there as well.

"Last year there was a major gas pipeline explosion in downtown Toronto; it closed up three blocks and it was caused by the erosion of one of the pipes. So if the right explosives are used, it will look like another natural gas fuck-up."

"Yes, yes!" said Jennie. "But what about Lisa? She'll be in the clubhouse, acting as one of the VIP hostesses. How will they get her?" No one could come up with a quick answer.

"Wait, I'll bet that someone will come into the clubhouse yelling that Sam is injured and get Lisa to take off with them," she said, answering her own question. "And that person will no doubt be a plant. Well, we'll just have to figure out how to keep her in my line of vision.

"Okay, I got it," Jennie continued after a moment of thought. "Grant, change my job description. I'll have to be a waitress – that way I can wander around the VIP area and no one will get suspicious.

"Yes, that will definitely work out the best," she repeated to herself. "David, you'll have to do security so you'll get to ride in that special golf cart that I've fantasized about for these past thirty minutes. Oh well."

Grant was overwhelmed with admiration and gratitude for Jennie's ability to balance her professionalism with her personal feelings. Seeing that Lisa was still here with him no doubt told Jennie all she needed to know. He had never felt confident sharing his personal feelings with anyone, but now he had to try. He walked over to her and took her arm.

"I can't think of the right words to say to you right now other than thank you," he whispered. "I have never learned how to share personal stuff. But I want you to know that for all of your life, wherever you are, if ever you need me, I will be there."

Jennifer's eyes started to fill, but she didn't answer him. Then she quickly got herself back to business as they both turned to face David.

"Now gentlemen, let us sit down and have a really good look at the layout of that golf course," said Jennie. "Thank the Lord for laptops and wireless. Let's pull it up and see what we have."

"Geez, what good am I doing here?" laughed David. "You guys have it all figured out."

An hour later Grant called Lantinos.

"What are you nuts?" mumbled Bob as he picked up the phone.

"Who me?" laughed Grant. "Nope. We need to make a small change in plans. David and Jennie are going to catch the first plane out of Orlando tonight, or today, or whenever it is, and stopover in Buffalo to meet with Brattini whom I just spoke to. After that they will go on to Toronto. They are going to stay at the Tranby house."

"And this news couldn't wait until the morning?" asked Bob. "I guess you have some information that you no doubt want to share with me. But I don't want you to, at least not right now."

"Right on," answered Grant. "I just wanted to keep you in the loop. Poor Jennie and David, along with me, have had no sleep for almost forty-eight hours."

"Boohoo," said Lantinos before he hung up the phone. "That's why I'm the boss and you aren't. Okay, you know where I am."

CHAPTER TWENTY-FIVE

Buffalo, New York.

Jennie and David spotted the man before he spotted them.

"They are so obvious," whispered Jennie as the two of them walked through the airport. "Navy suit, dark glasses, one hand in their jacket pocket. I feel like walking up to him and yelling 'boo!'"

"Well, that should get an interesting response," laughed David. "Okay, quiet, here he comes."

After the three of them all nodded to each other as if they were actors in a 1920's silent film, David and Jennie checked their luggage into a storage compartment. Their connecting flight to Toronto was leaving in just over an hour.

They followed Mr. Dark Glasses out to a navy-coloured Escalade. The back door opened, and when they got in there were two men inside.

The car pulled away and drove down what looked like a service road behind the terminal to a parking lot where it stopped. The light went on inside the back of the car and a glass barrier slowly closed off the two men sitting in the front.

"Giancarlo Brattini, it's so nice to finally meet you in person," smiled Jennie as she extended her hand. "I've watched you so often from so many different angles that I feel like I know you intimately."

David refrained from smiling, knowing that this experience was one that he would never be a part of again – and Jennie really was the best at playing the game.

"Ah Ms. White, it sounds like you actually have a personality," answered Johnny taking her hand. "How unique for someone who is in the cops and robbers business.

"And you must be Mr. Awasake," said Johnny extending his hand. "Welcome to my world." David nodded and noticed how powerful Brattini's hold was on his hand.

"And now, I would like to introduce both of you to Mario Lata, my friend and associate. He's in charge of our teams." Lata just nodded.

"We don't have much time to make sure that we get all our plans on the same page," Brattini continued. "Especially since I am going to be in Cleveland next weekend and will miss this once in a lifetime party in Toronto. But Mario will be there with you, sitting in my place."

Then their conversation took off and became animated as they started tossing around a couple of different scenarios. Johnny raised the question of identifying those whom he referred to as the bad guys.

"I think that your analysis of the actual assault is right on," he said to Jennifer. "And even though it dates me, I assume that the five Mohawk men will be easily identifiable so one of my two teams will be right on them – if we can locate them before the fact. The first question is whether there will only be the Mohawk team or if Latchman is bringing in some of his Sicilian goons? We need the answer to that question pretty soon."

"We also need to know who will be planting the explosives," said David, "or, if they are already planted, how they will be detonated. My ongoing concern is being able to figure out who is who."

"Well, my two teams will have different coloured hats that are wired for each," said Johnny. "I understand that your people are also sending in a couple of explosive sniffers. We've got to be sure that no one from the other side gets a hint that we're on to them or everything will be called off and we'll be back to square one."

"If your assessment is right Jennifer," Johnny continued, "and the plan is to have some sort of explosion under that highway overpass, my second team will already be hiding on site. By then they'll have gone over the whole area with electronic sniffers. There's so much foliage, bushes, trees and large rocks in that area that it's possible they could miss buried explosives. But hopefully, if the stuff is there, they'll find it.

"The way Latchman and Ramsay described their plans to me when we met a couple of days ago," Johnny went on, "is that they intend to get it all done in one day. That means all their guys will be there...somewhere. My guys are going in the day before and, since they have played the undercover game so many times, they'll be keeping out of sight. If we get lucky, they'll be able to get the goons, if and when they show up.

"And Jennifer, one more critical part of this is to keep the cops away," he said very forcefully. "You'd better speak to someone in your department about that. We don't need any gawking, clumsy cops walking into our line of vision and alerting Latchman's men."

"Yes, I'll do that," said Jennie. "Actually, I think Grant will be following it up."

"Obviously our first choice is that they just show up and come sauntering along," Johnny continued, "and if they think that no one knows what's going on, then they might just do that. But we aren't counting on it – too good to be true and all that."

"Gee Johnny, did you ever think of switching sides?" asked Jennie with a wide smile. "This unlikely and not-to-be-believed partnership could change the face of all future Godfather movies."

"Very funny," snapped Johnny. "I don't like this any better than you. But in this very unique circumstance, very unique responses are required."

David was enjoying their conversation and said nothing. Mario Lata hadn't moved or reacted to anything, and he looked like one of those zombies in horror movies.

"But," Johnny said with a smile as he continued, "given this new spirit of cooperation between us, perhaps you could take me on a tour of your new Lab 1? That is, if you're really serious about getting into bed together, figuratively speaking, of course."

How the hell does he know about Lab 1? thought Jennie – Lab 1 being a secret research facility under the umbrella of the FBI. *Shit, these guys are everywhere. Okay, no more games.*

Even at the very top level, it was too easy to slip into a bantering playbill with the bad guys. Tired people who are under pressure and want to lighten it up can talk too much.

Jennie was quiet as they arrived back at the terminal building. Johnny turned off the lights inside the car.

"My nephew, Peter DeLuca, is conducting an interview with Yuri Latchman as we speak," Johnny said. "I expect to have critical information by the time you've settled into Lisa's house in Toronto."

This was the first time Johnny had referred to Peter as his nephew.

That just popped out of my mouth, thought Johnny. *I guess this whole exercise is going to have a lasting effect on all of us.*

"You sound pretty sure of that," said David.

"I am," answered Johnny. Silence.

"Okay then, we will be counting on your team to neutralize the bad guys" said Jenny. "It's very important for us to be able to tell them apart."

"Oh don't worry," said Johnny, "you will." He tapped the glass partition twice and the navy suit jumped out and opened the back door.

"Have a good weekend with your family," said Jennie as she shook Johnny's hand. "I'm sure the Palozzo's will throw a party to end all parties in honour of Uncle Vincent's ninetieth birthday."

Shit, that broad knows everything, thought Johnny. *So much for secret family gatherings. She really is one of them.*

CHAPTER TWENTY-SIX

Boston, Massachusetts.

They were sitting in a small office just west of the Charlestown Community Centre. It was the front part of a large storage building that was used by DeLuca Industries to store the equipment needed to maintain the rental properties they owned. Peter DeLuca was sitting behind a desk; Lenny Brattuso was on a cane-backed chair against the wall.

Yuri Latchman was in a high-backed steel chair, straps holding his head back against the top, his arms and hands strapped along the chair's arms. His legs were spread open and also strapped against the chair. His eyes were still closed. He appeared to be sleeping but was, in fact, unconscious – a shot of ketamine had been put in the drink he had enjoyed earlier in DeLuca's downtown office.

He had been transported here wrapped in a burlap bag by the two men standing near the doorway. One was a tall, thin blond and the other was a Korean man. Latchman's body had just started to twitch, so he would probably be awake and alert in about five minutes.

Next to Latchman, also strapped into a steel chair was Silvana Rackova, executive assistant to Lenny Brattuso for the last seven years. She had a look of wild terror on her face and though she had a gag in her mouth, sounds still emanated from her.

"Silvana, how could you betray me like this?" asked Lenny. His eyes were cold and his tone was even colder. "I gave you a job. I gave you a condo. I treated you with respect. You of all people should have known what would happen to you for being a part of something like this."

She kept trying to move and sounds from her throat muffled through the gag.

"And with a Russian?" he went on. "Of course, now that I know that you are one of them, it is understandable. I do give you credit for learning Italian as well as you did. I never suspected for a second that you weren't actually from Friuli and one of my people. You even knew some local hot spots. But that was then, and this is now.

"I'm going to tell you what's going to happen next," continued Lenny. "So please concentrate. When I remove your gag you are going to tell me, step by step, how you diverted the payments of DeLuca Industries right under my nose; who helped you to do it, where you sent the payments, where they were deposited, how you were going to retrieve the money for Latchman, what phony documents and information you entered into the computer and the hard copy files and, finally, who else besides Latchman was involved with you.

"Just to be sure that you quickly and accurately answer my questions, you are now going to get a taste, but just a little taste, of what will happen to you if you hesitate even one second longer than needed to spit everything out."

Brattuso then nodded at the men. The blond man picked up a hammer lying on the floor. It was used to crumble drywall removed from buildings being renovated. He then walked over to Silvana and broke every finger on her left hand. Her eyes were almost totally back in her head and her stifled screaming and twitching body gave no comfort to Lenny as he pulled off the gag.

Her screams had become crying and moaning and coughing.

"I'm so sorry," she sobbed. "He told me he would get my mother out of Minsk."

"Seven years!" raged Lenny. "Why didn't you tell me about your mother? How could you betray me like this?

"Wait, don't bother answering me," Lenny continued before she could say anything. "I don't really care. Just start talking. After that you can relax and enjoy the rest of this show. And feel free to answer any questions that your friend here doesn't. You might earn some brownie points."

Latchman was now wide awake. His face was expressionless. Only his eyes turned to settle on Peter DeLuca, sitting quietly at the desk. And as they glared at each other the hate between them was electric.

"Yuri kept bragging about how you liked to give him blow jobs," said Peter as he turned away from Latchman to look at Silvana. "So I think that Lenny started on the wrong part of your body. He should have had your teeth knocked out first so you could service the Russian even better – no worries about bites."

"Well that assumes that Latchman is still going to have a cock and balls after the guys are finished with him," said Lenny. "And that isn't a good assumption."

Silvana started to howl again, begging for mercy and promising to do anything for them if they wouldn't hurt her again.

For the next twenty minutes Silvana answered all of Lenny's questions as he took notes. Peter listened with no expression. Latchman just glared.

"I can get most of what she has done reversed within a week," said Lenny as he turned to Peter. "Luckily Palona and two of his agents are en route to Sierra Leone. They can buy us some time to get our money back into the right hands. But first we have to know where Latchman specifically sent it. One of our questions that he will no doubt be happy to answer."

"Wait, I know where they were sent!" yelled Silvana in between sobs. Latchman started pulling at his bindings and began making guttural noises.

Lenny reached back and slapped him with a full frontal hand. Blood started pouring from his nose.

"Just outside of Herzliya is a small *kibbutz*," she said. "One of his agents lives there. Show me a map of the area, and I'll remember the name when I see it."

"Okay Yuri," said Peter as he turned back to him. "You fooled me for a very long time. It is interesting that Rebecca tried to talk to me about you so many years ago, but of course I was young and stupid and I didn't listen. How I wish I had.

"So now, we have come full circle. Our two friends here don't like Russians and for sure don't like Sicilians whom I understand are your team of choice. We are now going to leave you with them. Silvana is going stay on to be a witness on your behalf just in case this ever gets to court.

"You know the exercise, Yuri" Peter went on. "I want to know your specific plan for the twenty-fifth. I want to know where the explosion will take place and whether the explosives are preset or will be planted on the day of."

The look of shock on Latchman's face when Peter mentioned explosives confirmed that Jennifer White's gut instinct had been right on.

"I want to know how many men will be at the golf course. When are they getting there? What is the plan for grabbing the kid and his mother? Where will the Sicilians be holed up? The sooner you talk, the more of you will still be attached to your body. First they will use the blow torch. After that, the electric saw. Lenny and I are going out for dinner. Have a good time."

"No, no!" shrieked Silvana. "Don't leave me here to watch. Please, please!"

"Put a gag in her mouth," Lenny told the men. "She's earned the right to watch all of it."

Two hours later, Lenny and Peter sat in the Italian card club that had once been the favourite hangout of their fathers. They were drinking Napoleon brandy and were talking about the past – their fathers, their happy boyhoods – and what they believed to be their irrevocable destinies – following the path that they were born to. Neither one had any regrets or discomfort about what they had done in the past, what they were currently doing and where the road might take them in the future.

"After all these generations, I wonder if it's genetic," said Peter, almost laughing.

"Who knows?" said Lenny. "But one thing I do know for sure is thank the Lord that Matthew isn't around here. Maybe he is the gift your father offered to God to balance you...and me."

Lenny's phone began to ring. It was time for them to return to Silvana and Latchman.

When they got back to the building, the two men were waiting outside. Lars, the blond one, spoke first.

"He's still alive," he said. "But he won't talk. I've never seen anyone take this kind of punishment and not give up. This guy is made of stone. If we do anything more he'll certainly die, and he's definitely not going to sing.

"It was a good idea to let the woman watch," he continued. "She kept yelling Latchman's team has been up in Toronto for over two weeks. She knows because she paid them from the cash kept in a box in Latchman's safe. And she says she thinks there are also two Sicilians from New Jersey who are supposed to be showing up to detonate the explosives – stuff that they got at a border crossing.

"Well, there is a certain irony in this outcome," said Peter. "Latchman zippers it, and the dame sings. Well, I agree with you that we've gotten as much information as we ever will."

When Peter's car pulled up, he nodded to the two men standing by the door. "Finish the job," he said.

Lenny gave each of them an envelope and then both he and Peter got into the car.

"I'll call Johnny when I get back home," Peter said as the car pulled away. "We will both have to send our best guys to Toronto.

"I can't take a chance on being seen there so I have to count on you to take over and pick the right guys to do the job." Lenny nodded silently.

"Johnny is also in agreement with me that you should lead the way," Peter continued. "Mario Lata, Sal's son, is going to be there as well. I've never worked with him before – let's hope everything works out."

CHAPTER TWENTY-SEVEN

Toronto, Ontario.

The Tranby property was located in one of the trendiest areas of Toronto – Yorkville. It was a narrow three-story red brick house with an open staircase halfway down the front hallway. There was a powder room just inside the front entrance. The kitchen was modern, updated and easy to use. There was a deck off the back where a barbecue sat covered in protective rubber. A large living and dining room completed this level. The second floor had two large and one smaller bedroom. There was a full bathroom with a Jacuzzi and a small three-piece with a walk in shower. The third floor was the master suite – a huge bedroom and sitting room, used as a den. The bathroom was black and gray marble with a huge walk-in shower, a separate Jacuzzi, double sinks, a bidet and heated tiles. The basement was finished and had a large playroom, one bedroom with twin beds and a bathroom.

Faux paint and wallpaper were used to cover what had once been shabby and chipped walls. The floors had been bleached a maple colour and the rooms lightened with the use of sheer swags as window treatments. There were several posters from Posters International and lithographs along the hallway.

Lisa had been lucky that her tenants, two very friendly gentlemen who had come to Toronto to be married three years earlier, appreciated living in such a nice home and took special care of it.

They had decided to move to San Francisco which is why the home was now vacant.

Lisa and Grant arrived at around four o'clock on the Thursday afternoon. Just as they got inside the front door Grant's phone rang.

"Hey bro, it's me," said Larry. "I assume you got there okay and everything is in order. Just to let you know that Elizabeth, Sam, Kevin, me and my mother are going out for an early dinner and then we have tickets for *War Horse*. So I'll bring the boys home later around eleven o'clock. Elizabeth will be staying with me."

"Thank you for everything," said Grant. "Jennie and Awasake are still in Washington. Lantinos needed them to go back there to give a face-to-face report because Bartoli insisted. He wanted them to answer any questions up close and personal. I expect them here by tomorrow night."

"Okay, see you later," said Larry.

Grant and Lisa ordered in some Chinese food after they had unpacked, and then they settled down in the kitchen to eat and talk across the centre island.

"This is the first time in so long that I feel a bit more relaxed," said Lisa as she munched on her spring roll. "But that won't last for long. So let's talk."

Grant smiled and stretched his arms across the counter to take her hands in his.

"Where do we begin?" he asked. She looked at him and smiled.

"Hey, isn't that the opening line of a famous love story song? Who says you aren't a romantic?" said Lisa.

Her smile deepened and her dimples made him smile back.

"I want us to be together," said Grant, "starting right now. No more pretences – no more bullshit. Somewhere along the line during these past years, you have become a necessary part of my life – a part beyond being the mother of my son.

"I love being with you and Sam; I love coming to visit you and spending time relaxing and *kibitzing* around, and, of course, I really love our political debates. I now realize that I kept pushing away any passion I felt for you because it seemed so impossible – so inappropriate – and so I buried my feelings by always seeking other attractions.

"Now, I won't lie to you," Grant continued. "I have enjoyed the sexual relationships that I have had over the years. I sometimes asked myself why I never let any one of them get beyond the first stages, and now I know why. It was you, always you, underneath the surface…it was you.

"I loved Rebecca. And even though we didn't have much time together, she lit up my life. But it's almost fifteen years since she's been gone. Today there is you and me, and the dynamics of our chemistry is too incredible for me to let go.

"So that is it. I just want to tell you again, how much I love you, how much I appreciate the mother you have been and are to Sam, and to Kevin, and the special friend that you were to me back when I was floundering.

"Now you may speak."

Lisa looked at Grant silently for a few moments as her eyes filled with tears.

"You have never let me down. And along that line, I confess to having lewd and disgusting thoughts every time I look at certain parts of you."

Grant tried to give her his most sensuous leer. He missed, and she laughed.

"You were right in your assessment of my relationship with Isobel," Lisa continued, "she was there, she was confident, she loved me and I was hurting. I am lucky that she's the kind of woman that she is – she helped me get through the first years without my parents and without you.

"There is also no doubt that I had stronger feelings for you than I was willing to admit to myself for a long time," she went on, "and it's great for Sam and me to have you around. It's fun sharing so much of his life with you and I love being Mommy Lisa to Kevin.

"I didn't want to be a replacement for my mother," she continued. "I wanted to make sure that it was me you were looking at; not a memory of her. I believe that you love me, so whatever fate is now sending our way, I am confident standing next to you, knowing that you are protecting Sam and me, trusting in your judgement and most important, confident in your courage."

Grant and Lisa wrapped their arms around each other in silence. Then they spent the next two hours cleaning the house, each one bemoaning Grant's decision not to hire a cleaning firm. Beds had to be made, sheets and towels had to be laundered, washrooms had to be scrubbed and rugs vacuumed. Finally, at eight o'clock, the job was done.

"Okay," Lisa sighed, "time for a Jacuzzi and a bit of relaxation before Kevin and Sam get here." She walked over to Grant who was putting the garbage bags by the side door and tapped him on the shoulder.

"Hey big guy," she purred when he turned. She pushed her body against his. "Are you busy for the next hour? No? Have I got an offer for you, an offer that you can't refuse."

"Oh God, I love the way you do that," moaned Lisa as Grant rotated his penis inside her. He kissed her over and over again as he fondled her breasts, and when her nipples got hard, he lowered his head to suck on them. She called out his name as her body quickened and small shudders began to ripple through her. She lifted her legs and clutched his back as he buried himself deeper and deeper inside her and exploded.

"Mommy Lisa, Daddy, Daddy!" Kevin's calls jolted them awake. They had both dozed off "for just a minute" and both of them leapt out of the bed almost in unison.

"Shit, I don't have any clothes on," whispered Grant as he started pulling on sweatpants and a T-shirt.

"Thank God I have mine right here," said Lisa as she ran into the bathroom.

"Hey guys!" shouted Grant as he walked out onto the third-floor hallway. "Mom and I will be right down. Wait there for us!"

Grant was downstairs first as Kevin came running. They hugged and Grant gave him a huge kiss on his cheek that made him giggle.

Then came Sam – a hug that lasted a few seconds longer brought such a feeling of love over Grant than Larry with the usual warm hugs and pounding on the backs – and then, Elizabeth.

"Oh, how good it is to see you," said Grant as he hugged her. "I feel like the last week has been lived in outer space."

"Both of you have been in my thoughts," said Elizabeth as she kissed his cheeks. "And oh what fun I've had this week with Lyla. She and I might take our show on the road."

Larry burst out laughing as he winked at Elizabeth and she winked back.

"You can just imagine the two of them in action," Larry said to Grant. "Of course their conversation is mostly about girl stuff so I don't have to pay that much attention."

"Nice," said Elizabeth as she gave Larry a slight nudge and turned back to Grant. "We can chat about the important stuff when the boys are asleep."

Lisa came bounding down the stairs and joined the procession of hugs and kisses.

"Okay guys," she said to Sam and Kevin. "It's time for you to get to bed. Don't forget to say thank you and give Nonna Elizabeth and Uncle Larry big hugs for taking you out. Did you have fun?"

"Fantastic," answered Sam. "We had dinner at McDonalds; I had a Big Mac and so did Kevin. Then we went to the Ed Mirvish Theatre and saw *War Horse*. What a show! Kevin's eyes were glued to the stage the whole time and he wasn't fidgeting at all. It's something to think about – make sure you tell his school about that."

Grant smiled. "Thanks for letting me know Sam," he said. "I'll follow your advice."

"You boys will be sharing the downstairs bedroom," said Lisa. "We have so much to talk about and we will do that tomorrow after everyone has had a good night's sleep. Daddy and I are so tired after our long trip here all the way from Florida."

Grant and Lisa exchanged one of those eyes down, side glances that are instantly recognizable by other lovers. Elizabeth and Larry smiled at each other.

"Here are Kevin's pills," said Larry handing Grant the bottle. "He's been in great spirits and walking with Sam, Mom and me every morning."

"Hey, where is your mother?" asked Lisa. "I'm dying to meet her."

"I dropped her off after the play," answered Larry. "She wants to be in first-class condition when she meets you and Grant and she was very tired. She'll be here on Sunday."

It was close to eleven thirty by the time the kids were asleep and the four of them could sit down in the living room to catch up.

"Peter has kept me in the loop," said Elizabeth. "Or rather he has kept me in the limited loop that he chooses to share with me. And that's okay. I'm here, I'm ready, I'm not afraid and I'm determined to see us make it through."

"Well, this is the way it's going to have to play out," said Grant as he took Lisa's hand. "After the services at the cemetery on Sunday and the brunch that follows, I'm going to ask you and Larry to take Kevin out for a couple of hours. Lisa and I are going to tell Sam what is going on and that all of us, including him, are at risk."

Elizabeth sat up and moaned, "No, no, you can't do that. He's just a little boy." Of course she knew that she had described the baby he had once been – something so many grandmothers do so often.

"Look Elizabeth," said Lisa. "The hard and cruel reality is that he and I are going to have to be the bait. We have no other choice. But it will at least give us a chance for a future. What kind of life would we have if we were forever wondering when we would get shot or run over by a truck or just disappear?

"Thanks to the unbelievable skills of Jennifer White," she went on, "we now have a shot at screwing up the plans of Latchman and Ramsay. And with the backup of Johnny and Peter, it's possible to actually hope that we can get rid of those two yo-yos."

"I spoke to Lantinos just this afternoon," said Larry. "He is also feeling very confident, but his focus and the focus of his associates in Washington are on Latchman's Russian connection. Apparently he has a goon squad operating just outside of Kiev and, despite his claims of a personal friendship with the president, there is nothing to support it. As well, Bartoli heard that there are some plans to neutralize Latchman – at least that's what Bartoli's snitch is telling him.

"Lantinos also told me that last month Ramsay got careless about his Israeli connection in their finance ministry – the one who provides him with the forged letters of intent and powers of attorney. The PC subpoena accessed his email and to quote Jake, 'yahoo, their party is over!'"

"So everything is ready," Grant said. "We have tried to cover all possibilities. It now depends on a role of the dice. Let's hope we get lucky."

"If our plans work out," Grant continued, pulling Lisa's hand over to his mouth so he could kiss it, "Monday will be the last hurrah and the following weekend we will all be in Boston *shepping nachas* over Sam's bar mitzvah." Grant turned to Lisa and smirked as her face lit up.

"We wanted you to be the first to know that after that we are going to get married."

Larry and Elizabeth leapt out of their seats. It had been a long and winding twenty-year road for the four people who now stood together smiling, laughing, hugging and kissing each other. Their love for each other had sustained abuse, murder and betrayal. At this moment in time, they each savoured the feelings of joy, hope and confidence they were sharing.

CHAPTER TWENTY-EIGHT

It was ten o'clock on Sunday morning. Lisa Sherman, Sam Teasdale, Grant Teasdale, Kevin Teasdale, Larry Lyons and Elizabeth DeLuca walked together along the main pathway of the cemetery towards the grave of Rebecca Sherman. Once there, they were surrounded by a small group of friends and family – people who meant so much to them and who had once meant so much to Rebecca.

Buried next to Rebecca was Lisa's father, Steve. Their headstones were separate – they had been divorced – but Lisa knew that if there was another place in time, they would be content to be close together. Right behind their burial plots were those of Rebecca's parents, Naomi and Jack Singer.

Rabbi Michael Dolgin arrived to conduct the brief memorial service.

"Sam, come stand here with me," said the Rabbi taking his arm. "Lisa, you can stand next to your son.

"In Judaism, a newborn is named in honour of someone who is dead," he said. "That is how they are never forgotten – they live forever in the name of those who have come after them. There are some who believe that until a dead person has a name, they are destined to remain in limbo before they can move on to the next world.

"So you, Sam, are the living memory of your grandfather Steve; any time that your name is spoken, it is a remembrance of him as well. Today we have come to this sacred place to not only remember those we loved, but to invite them to join us at a very special milestone – your bar mitzvah.

"Tradition dictates that we say *neshama* while reciting the names of the deceased and then we follow up with *El Melay Rachamim*. Please join me."

After the prayer the Rabbi then said, "Please take a moment to remember the people we are here to honour in your own personal way."

Lisa stared at her mother's headstone in silence. She walked over and picked up a stone from the ground to put on the top.

I am standing here and I feel more pain about not having my father and grandparents. Where did you and I lose it Mom? I'll never know how things might have been had you lived – but then I wouldn't have Sam. Forgive me for loving Grant. He is everything I will ever want or need. Please protect Sam. Rest in peace.

Elizabeth then walked up to Rebecca's headstone and put her hand on it.

Oh Rebecca, Rebecca. How strange that we reached out to each other so long ago. And we became more than friends – we were the guardians of each other's bodies and souls, compadres, sisters by choice and not by blood.

If not for your presence, first in Santino's life and then in mine, my sons and I would have been ruined. And if not for your courage and your loyalty, I doubt that my sons and I would still be alive.

We never had a chance to say goodbye. I miss you so much. And oh how I wish you could have lived to see Sam. He is everything you could have ever hoped for in a grandson.

So if you are somewhere and can read my thoughts, know that I am here for Lisa and Sam for all of their lives. Rest in peace my dear friend.

Then it was Grant's turn. He took Sam's hand as he lifted two stones from the ground and put them on Rebecca's headstone.

Oh how I loved you – about that you can have no doubt. If you are somewhere and can read my thoughts, I hope you are not angry with me for falling in love with your daughter. I see so much of you in her. I wish you knew how courageous she has been during this crisis. She reminds me of you.

I will take care of her, and of Sam, for all of my life. Rest in peace, my darling Rebecca.

Brunch was still being enjoyed when Jennifer White and David Awasake arrived at the Tranby house. They were welcomed with quiet cheers and hugs and pats on their backs.

"Bagels, lox, herring and chopped eggs," cooed Jennifer. "I haven't had this kind of banquet for so long. Excuse me while I fill my plate."

"Ah ha," said Lyla Leone as she walked over to Jennifer with a big smile on her face. "I knew that you were too smooth and too gorgeous and too sexy to really need my services.

"So I am delighted to get a chance to meet you again, with my boy Larry alive and well and back in the life of his mother," she went on. "Thank you for being a part of those trying to reunite us. It has been like a dream. I am so lucky and oh so proud."

Larry was standing against the wall, smiling as he listened to his mother.

"Ms. Leone, I am so honoured to meet you in this environment," said Jennifer. "Your story is the kind that helps us get through all the others with bad endings. It reflects our hope and faith.

"And now I would like to introduce you to my partner, David Awasake."

Jennie reached over and grabbed David's jacket as she pulled him over to face Lyla.

"Oh, aren't you interesting," said Lyla with a big smile filling her face as she took his hand. "And what do you do in your spare time?"

"Mom, cut it out!" laughed Larry. "You promised to behave."

And on that note of fun and optimism, the next two hours passed quickly.

"Kevin and I are going to the museum today," said Larry as they got ready to leave.

"And Elizabeth and I are going to have a spa afternoon," Lyla piped in. "We have to make sure that we'll be ready for next week's Boston celebrations."

"Well, this looks serious," said Sam as he sat down opposite his parents in the living room.

"It is," answered Grant. "And at the outset, let me tell you that both your mother and I will respect whatever decision you make. If you need extra time to think it over, that's okay."

"Are you giving me up for adoption?" asked Sam with a straight face.

Both Grant and Lisa burst out laughing.

"Okay, we get your point," said Grant. "Here we go."

"Your grandmother Rebecca was involved with Santino DeLuca and his business for many years," Grant began. "Now I know that you have read about this on the internet and you are quite knowledgeable about the kind of business that he was in."

"And the rest of the family as well," said Sam, "including Uncle Johnny. Anyhow, I really don't care what they did. You both should know my favourite expression by now. I use it more often than not when I am dealing with some of the nerds at school."

"And what expression is that?" asked Lisa.

"'Let those of you who are without sin, cast the first stone,'" he answered.

"I know it's not exactly a part of my religion," Sam continued with a smile, "but it sure is effective, especially when bullies are trying to justify their actions."

"Well, over the last fifty years, there were fights and business screw ups and murders that happened," said Grant. "People who were once friends became enemies, and they began trying to outdo each other in the payback department, and pretty soon it was hard to remember what it was that happened in the first place. It all became just a game of payback."

"That's what goes on at Boston Latin," said Sam. "Somebody gets insulted, tries to pay back whoever caused it, somebody else offers to help, and before you know it, there's a fight and nobody's sure who's who."

Grant looked at Lisa for a few moments and then spoke again.

"Sam, there is going to be an attempt to harm you and your mother. The reason has nothing to do with either of you – it has to do with things that happened years and years ago – things that involved three people who are now dead: Uncle Johnny's father, Massimo, Uncle Peter's father, Santino, and your grandmother, Rebecca.

"The people wanting to hurt you are not normal," Grant continued. "They've been dysfunctional for so long that they wouldn't know how to do the right thing even if they wanted to.

"Uncle Larry is a key player in this scenario. Jennifer White and David Awasake, who you met at brunch today, are also key players in helping to eliminate the danger to you and your mother."

"In other words, they are trying to get the bad guys before they get us," said Sam.

Again, Grant and Lisa just looked at each other. This time they shared a smile.

"Yes, that's true," said Grant. "The only way they can do that is if you, and your mother, show up at where they think you'll be. And when they try to get you, we'll be there waiting to get them."

"What if Mom and I just don't go?" asked Sam.

"Then they'll find another time and place to try to get you."

"So if we don't stand up now," said Sam, "it will keep following us – the threat that is."

Then Sam turned to his mother.

"What do you think Mom?"

"Dad and I want you to help us make the decision," she answered. "I'm certainly a bit frightened, who wouldn't be? But I'm ready to do whatever's needed, and with your father right beside us, we have the best protection."

"What is their plan?" asked Sam. "When and where is this supposed to happen?"

He appeared to be very interested and was showing no fear. *Maybe he doesn't understand what is going on here,* thought Lisa.

"Tomorrow – at the golf tournament," answered Grant.

"What?" yelled Sam, "I hope that you haven't arranged this drama on purpose, Dad, simply because you don't want to lose to me, which you definitely will!"

Grant almost broke down, something he hadn't done since Rebecca's death. *What a blessing this boy is. How can I be so lucky?*

Lisa put her hand on her mouth, not wanting to lose her composure.

"What will I have to do?" asked Sam after he realized that neither of his parents could speak.

"Nothing," choked Grant. "You just have to behave as you would normally. We will both be together and there will be others hidden on the course who will be watching out for you as well."

"Sam," Lisa said before the tears started. "You don't have to do this. We can move away or hope the police can figure out a way to get these guys."

"Forget that, Mom," answered Sam. "I don't want to be looking over my shoulder all of my life.

"Hey, will I get to wear a bullet proof vest?"

"Actually, yes," answered Grant, "and so will I and so will your mother.

"There is one other critical fact that you have to know before we show up tomorrow," said Grant. "The men that we are playing golf with are also bad guys. We can't let them know that we know that, but it's critical that you're aware of it just in case something unexpected happens."

"But isn't it the Mayor who is playing with us because Mr. Ramsay has no son?" asked Sam.

When Grant didn't answer, Sam just nodded. *His first disillusionment*, thought Lisa. *There will be so many more throughout his life.*

"Okay," said Sam. "I am a bit scared, but not that much. Maybe that's because Dad will be right there with me." Then he turned to Lisa.

"Let's do it, Mom. I'm ready."

CHAPTER TWENTY-NINE

Toronto Valley Golf Course.

Lisa arrived at the club with two other volunteer hostesses at one o'clock. She was wearing a Donna Karan outfit that she had bought at Holt Renfrew the day before. The pants were linen and the top was a loosely draped multicoloured silk – it covered the bulletproof vest underneath. She was given an ID card and told to wear it around her neck before she was directed to the reception table. Her job was to pass out the refreshment tickets and make sure that each foursome was marked off on their arrival and that they had the right directions to the hole from which they were assigned to tee off. Sitting next to Lisa was Cindy Ashton, the Mayor's wife.

    The clubhouse had only one entrance. Normally, golfers could walk down a steep hill to the first tee without going inside the clubhouse, but given that a US senator was also going to be in attendance, security blocked access to that hill today. Next to the reception area was the dining room which was now set up with flowers and a bar.

    Working there were staff only, and Lisa was very happy to notice Jennie's presence. She was wearing a uniform that had black pants covering the gun taped on her ankle and a white tunic top. She had a large white rose in her hair. It was actually an electronic device that was in the developmental stage – it picked up sound and was also a mini camera. The room was being set up and all the paperwork was being prepared for the golfers who would start arriving at two o'clock. Once registered, they could go into the dining room to get a drink or a snack. After the tournament ended, a buffet dinner would be served followed by speeches and the passing out of prizes for those golfers with the best scores.

The weather was perfect – seventy-two degrees and sunny with a light breeze that rustled through all the trees and foliage. All the views were spectacular.

When Mayor Carl Ashton and Deputy Minister Howard Ramsay arrived at the club, the camera flashes started going off. There were several media outlets present including some who were opposed to the kind of public spending that an event such as this cost.

Ten minutes later, Grant Teasdale arrived with his son, Sam. Both were wearing matching Polo shirts and cashmere cardigans. The sizes were larger than they usually wore in order to make sure that the bullet proof vests they were wearing couldn't be seen.

There was a box of golf hats that had been donated by Golf Town for all the players. Grant quickly found two on the very bottom that had happy face buttons and picked them up. The buttons were GPS devices used to keep their location known. Sam had the earplugs from his iPhone on, ostensibly to listen to music, but in reality a walkie-talkie – something Johnny Brattini had customized for him as soon as he got back to Buffalo, which he then had delivered to Lisa's house earlier that morning. This would keep Sam within reach.

Lisa smiled and then introduced them to the Mayor's wife who was sitting next to her.

"Oh, what a handsome boy," said Mrs. Ashton as she smiled at Sam. "What is your handicap?"

"Oh, I don't keep score," answered Sam as his father smiled. "I just like to have a good time."

Grant leaned over and whispered, "Just remember your words Sam my boy, especially when you lose."

THE THIRD HOLE

Larry was trying to stay as invisible as possible by wearing a hard hat marked "City of Toronto" and a jumpsuit with the city logo on the front. If his presence ever became public, it would require a very awkward explanation which is why he was sitting in one of the City trucks usually parked under the 401 highway overpass just past the 1st hole and in front of the 18th tee.

To some avid golfers, the never ending construction going on there was a slow torture. Two years earlier, there had been two deaths attributed to that bridge; one man had jumped off and the other was a young woman who was found dead in the bushes, also a suspected suicide.

In addition to Larry, there were two other teams on the course. DeLuca's men, led by Lenny Brattuso, were wearing gray golf hats turned backwards. They had ear pieces and were carrying Kalashnikovs – easily held and easily hidden. They were up on the side of the hill under the overpass that was covered by bushes and trees that were in full bloom. The site had already been checked for buried explosives and none had been found. It was always possible they had been missed, but the strategy now in place was that a pair of Sicilian dogs, as DeLuca liked to call them, would show up in some disguise to set up the fireworks and then take off.

Over by the 3rd hole, Brattini's men, under the direction of Mario Lata, were also spread out on both sides of the hills – much higher than the others around the course. These men were wearing wired black golf hats and zoom lenses disguised as sunglasses, which allowed them to get a better view through the trees. They were carrying Glock semi-automatic handguns as well as assault rifles. No one was exactly sure what they would be facing.

In this location there was also a large man-made lake surrounded by trees and walking paths for anyone who wanted to use it. There was also a square building made out of gray stones that was used as a water storage centre by the municipality. The foliage around there was even denser, and it ran all the way up another large hill that overlooked the hole on one side and the main road leading to the club on the other side.

All of the men, and Jennie, were connected by radio transmitters so they all heard whatever was being spoken by any of them. It was newly developed in Lab 1.

The entire golf course, especially the area surrounding the 3rd hole, was set in a deep ravine. The houses that overlooked the course sat on top of the hill and if a resident walked to the edge of their property line they would have an excellent view of the course below, including the pathways to and from the 3rd hole. They were also at the same height as the top of the hill across the fairway, though they couldn't see beyond the top and over into the city itself.

Marilyn and Mel Masterson had just settled onto their matching lounges located next to their pool. Their property was located at the top of the highest hill on the south end of the 3rd hole and from there they had unfettered views all around, including the fairways on the 4th hole and the hills on both sides of the 3rd hole's green. From their vantage point they often watched small animals chase each other up and down the sides. They had even spotted a pair of hedge hogs with a baby working their way up the hill.

Suddenly they were surrounded by several men, two of whom were wearing ski masks.

"How did you get in here?" bellowed Mel before he realized what a stupid question that was. "What do you want?" he asked a little more gently.

"We are not going to cause you any harm," answered the voice behind one of the masks. "We must use this space for the next few hours and so we will have to ask you to step back inside. Again, we will cause you no physical harm as long as you cooperate."

By now Marilyn was whimpering. One of the masks nodded to his men who then escorted the couple back inside to their bedroom. They were given bathroom privileges, supervised by one of the men, and then they settled down. The TV was turned on for them to watch CNN. Once they were out of sight, Johnny Brattini took off his ski mask.

THE THIRD HOLE

Johnny had known from the outset that he would have to be here himself. He couldn't take a chance on someone making a mistake – a mistake that could cost Sam and Lisa their lives.

"Okay, we can see everything from here," he said to Mario Lata as both men checked out the views.

"Can any of you see any windows on neighbouring properties where someone could look out and spot us?" asked Brattini.

"I don't think so," answered Mario. "Paolo, can you see anything?"

"Nope," answered one of the men setting up equipment next to the pool.

"I just connected with my guys on the other side of the hill," said Mario. "They're now in place."

"I know this is all kind of unusual," said Johnny. "But this is an unusual situation. And remember, the guys with gray hats on backwards are part of this team. The only ones we are interested in are the five Mohawks and the two Sicilians."

Then David Awasake took off his ski mask and unravelled a large fabric bag. Out came a Métis war bonnet – something that represented the highest of respect for the person who owned it. This one was made of eagle feathers, a bird viewed by the Métis as one of the most sacred. Each feather represented a good deed or a brave act. The one in David's hands had fifty feathers on it.

Johnny stared at it without saying a word. Then he looked up at David who smiled at him and said, "We're having a war dance, are we not?"

Johnny burst out laughing and shook his head.

"What time is it?" asked David.

"Almost three o'clock," answered Mario.

"Okay – here we go."

Sam stood behind his father as Grant drove off the first tee. The ball had to cross a stream in order to reach the fairway.

"Good shot," said Sam as he pulled his driver out of his bag. He smiled at Howard Ramsay and Mayor Ashton sitting in their cart.

"Hey Sam, how can you concentrate on your golf if you're listening to music with those things on the top of your head sticking in your ears?" asked Ramsay.

"It's a lesson on doing two important things at once," answered Sam as he leaned over to put his ball on the tee. "Besides, it is a distraction from all the construction going on here and the noise of those drills just over our heads."

Sam brought his club back slowly, kept his head down and his eyes glued on the ball and let it go. The ball flew almost one hundred seventy-five yards away in a straight line towards the hole. Both Ramsay and Ashton's first shots had gone into the water.

"Are you guys going to take another shot from here?" asked Grant as he patted his son on the shoulder and the two other men applauded.

"No, we're going to play according to the rules," answered the Mayor. "We'll take a penalty shot from the other side of the water."

Back in the clubhouse, Lisa was making sure that all those names on the guest list had been properly checked off and were where they were supposed to be. Cindy Ashton was like her shadow, never moving more than ten feet away. When Lisa joined two other women to help display the flowers and make sure all the prizes were properly marked, Cindy trailed right behind.

She's so obvious, thought Jennie as she continued to set the tables and stack the place cards.

Jennie didn't buy into Cindy being the only watchdog for Lisa. She suspected there would also be professional backup in case Mrs. Honourable Mayor didn't do her job. Since Lisa was critical to Ramsay's plans for money laundering and murder, he wouldn't risk blowing it all with only an amateur. She figured there would have to be someone else in this room, or soon to be in this room. Jennie walked around filling water glasses, taking her time to turn all the menus in the proper direction and lining up the chairs around each table evenly.

Finally, she saw her. Ostensibly another waitress, one whose eyes kept flicking around the room as though she were looking for someone. Her head kept moving as she was obviously checking everything out. Her mistake, as often happens, was that she was wearing a uniform too tight for her body weight, and Jennie quickly saw the outline of what could be a gun in her apron.

Jennie knelt down to pick up some menus that she had casually pushed off a table just as that waitress came by. At the right moment, she quickly stood up and knocked the woman down. In the confusion that followed, Jennie rolled her part way under the table, behind the table skirt, and put her hand inside the apron's pocket. She pulled out the gun hidden there.

"One sound and you are dead," whispered Jennie just as she landed a karate chop on the side of the woman's neck that knocked her out. She then slipped the gun into her own apron.

"Oh, we need some help here!" Jennie called out as she pulled the woman out from underneath the table. "I tripped on this table skirt and the two of us took a terrible fall."

Lisa turned and looked over at Jennie before she looked down at the unconscious woman. *Why do I absolutely know that this has something to do with me?*

Two golf pros came running and called 911. They carried the woman out to the foyer to wait for an ambulance.

"Oh, I'm so sorry," whimpered Jennie to the club manager. "I don't understand how this happened."

Ten minutes later everyone in the clubhouse had settled down; the waitress was en route to the hospital and Jennie walked over to Lisa. Cindy Ashton had just left to go into the powder room.

"By any chance, do you know how to use a gun?" Jennie quietly asked her.

"No," answered Lisa, trying to stay calm.

"Well, I'm putting one in your shoulder bag. The safety lock is off." Lisa didn't say anything but the colour drained from her face.

"Just in case something unexpected happens," Jennie went on, "take it out, point it at the bad guy, and shoot. You've seen enough movies and TV shows to know where the trigger is. And after that, point it at the next bad guy and shoot again. You can do that eight times."

Do not burst out crying, thought Lisa as she just stared at Jennie. *Suck it up.*

The 2nd hole at the Toronto Valley Golf Course was flat and narrow. This time Howard Ramsay actually hit a good drive, sending the ball close to two hundred yards down the left side of the fairway. Sam had another excellent drive that landed only twenty yards behind his father, who was twenty yards behind Ramsay.

"Not bad," said Sam as he got into the cart. "Now all you have to do is lift your next shot high enough to miss the traps and you can be on the green in two. Of course, then you'll have to make a good putt – not that easy at your age."

Grant burst out laughing. Ramsay and Ashton looked back and were pleased that everything was going as planned. After all, Teasdale wouldn't be laughing if he had any idea what was coming.

Larry saw them first, coming over at the edge of the overpass just north of the 1st hole. He signalled to Lenny. The highway had a small maintenance exit just past the bridge so that workmen could access it without creating a major traffic problem. Larry quickly sent texts to his men who were cruising along the highway between the two major exits on either side of the club. He knew that it wouldn't take them more than a minute or two to arrive and quietly cut off any escape route.

Lenny Brattuso signalled his team over the radio: "The Sicilians have landed." The two men started sliding down the embankment; Lenny and Larry whispered to each other that they were not carrying anything visible, which meant that their weapons had to be pistols and the explosives must already be in place somewhere and very well hidden.

"Well Dad, what a surprise," laughed Sam as Grant made his birdie. "And congratulations Mr. Mayor for making yours."

"Gee Sam, maybe you'll get luckier on the next hole," said Grant as he pushed Sam's arm.

Lenny was now having second thoughts about laying low. "I would rather grab those guys and work on them quickly to get the information we need," he said to Larry. "They could have set this up with a detonator of some kind."

"Yes, but then that would mean they're suicide bombers," Larry said with a smirk. "And I doubt that. No, I think they're going to put the finishing touches on wherever the explosives are and then take off before the boom.

"And as we continued to sit in these maintenance trucks," he continued, "those Sicilians must have planned an alternate route out. But I can't figure out where that might be. Security has closed off the roadway."

Johnny stood up and adjusted his goggles as he watched the foursome of Grant and Sam Teasdale and their playing partners, Mayor Carl Ashton and Deputy Minister Howard Ramsay, approach the 3rd hole. The foursome in front of them were having a difficult time moving their shots in a timely manner. To an experienced golfer, it looked like a ten minute wait, which in the world of golf is a long time.

Mario, standing just off to the side, alerted his men hidden in the foliage on both of the hills that the foursome of interest was about five minutes away from teeing off. So far there had been no signs of anyone else hiding besides themselves – and Johnny was on edge.

Where the fuck are those Mohawks?

David Awasake had his binoculars focused on the surrounding area to the south. The wind had just started to pick up.

Grant Teasdale walked up to the tee at the 3rd hole. As he had just sunk a birdie putt on the last hole, he was the first off the tee. In front of him was a formidable challenge. There were several slopes on both sides of the fairway; the ideal landing spot was right on top the small hill directly in front of the tee. One hundred fifty yards would do it for the drive. The slightest miss and the ball would careen all the way down to the next hole on the right, or down to a man-made lake on the left. Whoever designed this hole must have been a frustrated bureaucrat.

There were only twenty yards of forgiveness and beyond that on either side were sand traps, bushes, tree trunks and, of course, the water – one could never forget the water.

Grant drove the ball beyond the top of the first hill, but he got a bad bounce and the ball rolled down the left side towards the water. Luckily, it caught in a brush and stopped just in front of the water's edge.

I'll have to use my wedge to chip it out of there, he thought when he saw the lie of the ball.

Sam, on the other hand, also drove his shot straight up the hill, but it had stopped, and though he still had over two hundred yards to go to the green, it was at least a clear, straight shot.

Grant had noticed a significant change in both Ramsay and Ashton as they approached the hole. Both men had gotten out of their cart and were standing next to each other, just looking at him. *Two pigs swimming in shit* was the expression in Grant's head.

"Come on guys," he said to them. "It's your turn. We don't want to hold anyone up."

"There's no one behind us," said Ashton. "We're the last foursome, so we can take some extra time or even an extra shot if we like."

Their tee shots were erratic. One hit a tree and landed in the rough.

"Take another shot," said Grant. "That one's gone."

"No, I'll try to find it first," answered the Mayor.

Ramsay's shot was almost a carbon copy of Grant's tee shot. In fact, Ramsay tried very hard to duplicate its landing, and he did – his ball rolled down the side of the hill and stopped about five yards away from Grant's ball.

As the Teasdale foursome came over the hill, Johnny noticed them through his goggles.

"Keep watching the hills," he said to Mario. "I'll stay focused on Sam's group."

Sam was standing next to his ball, trying to decide whether to use his three or five wood. He turned to look over at his father and ask for his advice when he saw, at that very moment, Ramsay's hand come down on Grant's neck as he then collapsed. Ramsay had injected him with ketamine, a channel blocker that paralyzes the muscles while the victim stays fully conscious.

"Enjoy yourself for a while," whispered Ramsay as he leaned over Grant's face.

Johnny saw it all too. "Teasdale's down!" he yelled into the transmitter. "Sam! Ashton is coming up behind you. Take off your hat and start running straight ahead."

"Hey, Sam!" yelled the Mayor. "Wait, let me show how your next shot can keep your ball in line for the hole!"

He came up right behind Sam's back. Sam pulled off this hat, grabbed his five wood and held it like a baseball bat as he turned around and swung, catching Ashton in a full frontal. Teeth flew and blood started running.

"Okay, good boy!" yelled Johnny as a smile came over his face. "Get going. Can you see that building over to your left by the hill?"

Sam yelled "yes" as he started to run towards it. Neither one of them needed to yell. The audio was working perfectly.

"Run around to the left side of the building and start scaling up the hill," said Brattini. "There are lots of trees so it'll be hard for anyone to see you, but I can see your red hair from up here. There are some deep holes in the ground, but I'll direct you around them."

Johnny turned to Mario. "Start working your way down to the kid," he said. "And send two guys over to Teasdale. Ramsay has to keep him alive, at least for a while."

Jennie froze as she listened to all the dialogue. She looked around the clubhouse and saw that everything was in order and nobody else knew what was going on. It took her only a few minutes to decide that she would hijack someone's golf cart and get over to the 3rd hole. *What about Lisa? I can't leave her here alone.*

Larry Lyons also heard everything and froze, but only for a moment. He turned to Brattuso and told him to stay alert and take charge. Larry was leaving and he was taking the truck.

Sam was running as fast as he could, all the while listening to Johnny's directions on where to turn and when to start crawling up the hill. He knew his father hadn't been shot – there had been no blood – and his eyes were open when Sam had looked over at him. He thought that Ramsay was holding a needle in his hand; Sam had read enough crime stories, seen enough movies and played enough video games to know what that could mean. *Freeze them up – paralyze their muscles – zap their brains! No, not my Dad. Not my Dad!*

Awasake heard the sound before he actually saw where it was coming from. But he knew instantly what it was. A helicopter!

"Holy Fuck!" he yelled as the rotors of the Sikorsky Pave Hawk helicopter appeared on the rise just above the hill. "The Mohawks are landing!"

"Keep your head down Sam!" yelled Johnny as he watched the red hair crawling up the side of the hill below him. "One of my guys is edging down to meet you. Keep yourself spread out as flat as you can, and don't turn to look at the noise just behind you. It's a helicopter and we don't want anyone to see you!"

After a few minutes of circling the area around the water, causing great waves and blowing sand, four men in bodysuits and goggles carrying C8s with suppressors wrapped over their shoulders started lowering themselves towards the ground with repelling cables attached to the helicopter.

Awasake said nothing to Johnny as he grabbed his fabric bag and started towards their landing spot.

The helicopter moved to the west and hovered after the men touched ground. Before they finished unhooking their cables, they all looked up and then froze. Standing tall in front of them was an aboriginal warrior wearing a war bonnet made of eagle feathers.

It was something they would have all learned about and seen pictures of when they were kids but not necessarily have come close to in real life. The war bonnet was something that epitomized for all of them what had once been the glory days of their ancestors – and for just a moment, they hesitated.

That was all it took. Six men, all of them a part of the Salerno crime family out of Buffalo and all loyal to Giancarlo Brattini, suddenly became visible as they stood up beside the trees on the left and quickly emptied their assault rifles into what had once been Yuri Latchman's specially trained war toys. They were all dead before they hit the ground.

David Awasake, a proud descendant of the once powerful Métis nation, a proud Mountie, and a very proud Canadian, then pulled out a LAW rocket launcher from his bag. As the helicopter turned to pull away, he carefully steadied the launcher on his shoulder and then fired at the helicopter's rear rotor. His aim was perfect and the helicopter spun up and around and then flipped over and down into the large ravine next to the fairway. There was little noise as the flames quickly engulfed everything except the fuel tank, which was happily immersed in the water surrounding the 3rd hole.

Johnny grabbed Sam just as Mario dragged him to the top of the hill.

"It's my Dad," sobbed Sam as the tears started to flow and Johnny held him tight. "We have to go back and get him."

Ramsay knew that he was in trouble. Ashton was lying with his face covered in blood twenty yards down the fairway and Ramsay had a clear visual of the helicopter and its destruction. What was supposed to be a quick and easy landing – picking up Lisa and the kid and his men on the ground and then flying them all back to Manitoulin Island while everyone else was running around trying to manage the gas explosion by the 1st tee – had simply not happened.

Where the fuck was that explosion?

Ramsay turned to look at his arch enemy, the one who had protected Rebecca Sherman for so long. Teasdale's eyes were open and his brain was working, but the rest of him was still paralyzed.

"Oh how you must be hurting," said Ramsay as he sneered at Teasdale. "Don't know where your kid is? Don't know if he's alive? Suffer, you rat."

Back at the 1st tee, the Sicilians had easily made their way over to the sand trap between the water and the cart path. It was hidden by the huge maple trees surrounding it.

That's where it's buried, thought Lenny. *Right in front of our noses. In the sand trap. It's only about ten yards from the main gas line – that must be it. It's probably C4 or that other explosive the terrorists use, Semtex. It must be buried in a plastic container. They could have a wireless remote or a battery operated pager. If they do have a detonator power source, anyone within thirty to forty feet is dead. And that means all of us.*

"Okay guys," said Lenny into what seemed to be the air. But everything was being transmitted clearly to everyone wearing the specially made hats with buttons – another new gizmo from Lab 1.

"There's too much open space to catch them by surprise. I'm going to have to gamble that it's buried in the sand. Izzy, do you have your rifle with you? Don't bother answering me. Use it if you can get a good enough shot at each of them."

Ten minutes later both Sicilians were dead. Standing around them were six men, all part of the Villano crime family out of Boston, and all loyal to Peter DeLuca.

This three month saga of murder and revenge had ended. Izzy had his head pounded by happy colleagues as they quickly dug up and diffused two large explosive devices that would have severed the gas supplies to a large part of the city's population. It would also have been a diversionary tactic, enabling the kidnapping and ultimate murder of Lisa Sherman and her son Sam Teasdale – but not before they had been tortured into signing some documents. The two Sicilians were placed in tarpaulins to be removed from the course later when it was dark and then dumped in some waste disposal unit.

Well, it actually had not ended...yet. Jennie and Lisa were speeding towards the 3rd hole in a golf cart Jennie had commandeered from the pro shop. Larry Lyons was in a city maintenance truck also speeding towards the 3rd hole. Johnny Brattini, who had told the world that he would be in Cleveland this weekend to preclude any repercussions from other families over this episode, was racing along the 3rd fairway with Sam Teasdale and David Awasake right beside him.

And still the rest of the golf course was operating as usual. Other than Marilyn and Mel, who were now being released after giving their promise of secrecy as they were accepting a brown manila envelope with twenty-five thousand dollars in cash, nobody else seemed to be aware of anything. It was still a day being enjoyed by the golfers.

Ramsay quickly walked back to his cart and drove it over to the water's edge where Grant was lying against a tree trunk. He pulled him partially up onto the seat and stood next to him. He put his left arm around his neck. In his right hand he held a syringe. He was ready.

He didn't have to wait long.

"This is cyanide!" yelled Ramsay as Larry got out of the truck and started towards him. To the left, Johnny, David and Sam stopped running and started walking towards him as well.

"One wrong move and I'll inject the poison directly into his carotid artery. He'll be dead before you can pull the trigger!"

"What do you want?" asked Larry. "You have nowhere to hide."

"Oh yes I do," answered Ramsay. "But first I want the money. And that means that Sherman's daughter has to sign the document I have in my pocket."

Jennie and Lisa were now visible coming up the fairway in another golf cart.

"Sam, are you okay?" called Lisa when she got out and started walking towards her son.

"Forget that!" yelled Ramsay. "If you want to see Teasdale alive for more than another fifteen seconds, you had better come over here and sign a piece of paper."

"I don't care one way or another about Teasdale," said Lisa with a smile. "He was my mother's boyfriend. But I care about my son, and he will never get over seeing his father murdered right in front of his eyes. So how about you let Sam start walking to the clubhouse and then I'll come over to you and sign your paper?"

Ramsay smiled. "What, do I look like a fool?" he sneered at her. "No, if you really care about your kid seeing his father zapped here and now, then you will do exactly what I say. Come over here and sign this paper, then I'll let him go."

Everyone stood in silence.

"All right," Lisa finally said. "I'll do it."

She started to walk towards Ramsay and when she was still a few yards in front of him she asked if he had a pen. He said that he didn't know but didn't want to start fishing for one.

"That's okay," she answered with a smile. "I'm sure that I have one in my purse."

Oh fuck, fuck! She's really going to do it! Jennie knew that she couldn't reach down to get the Beretta out of her leg holster without Ramsay noticing. She also knew that Ramsay could kill Grant before she could kill him. So she stood still and tried to remember all her prayers from Sunday school.

Lisa opened the zipper on her shoulder bag. She kept her eyes on Ramsay and the smile on her face as she put her hand inside the bag and started rummaging through it as she continued walking towards him.

"God, remind me to put my pen in a compartment in the future," she said, "then I won't have to keep clumping around inside looking for it."

"That's okay," said Ramsay, "take your time."

Lisa didn't think too much about anything when her hand closed on the gun's handle and her forefinger found the trigger. She was now less than ten feet away. She kept walking until she suddenly stopped, pulled out the gun and aimed it at Ramsay's head. For her, it was the easiest target on his body. She couldn't possibly shoot at his hand that was holding the syringe – she would miss for sure – and she couldn't get his lower body because he was holding Grant in front of him.

Oh well, here goes. Mommy, please help me!

She fired three times and was almost knocked over herself by the recoil. Ramsay, along with a large portion of his skull, fell backwards into the water. The syringe dropped from his hand.

It was over – it was finally over.

CHAPTER THIRTY

Boston, Massachusetts.

Temple Beth Israel was decorated with white mums. Lisa loved those flowers and made sure that the entire sanctuary looked like a country side in bloom.

This was the day of Sam Teasdale's bar mitzvah, a ritual that was a very special event for the Jewish people. It was the crossing over into manhood for their sons, and the beginning of their journey into life.

Sam was wearing a black robe over his new suit. He was nervous – he had to admit it. Like most bar mitzvah boys, he didn't know most of the people sitting behind him. But for those he did know, his parents, his brother Kevin, his great aunts and uncles, the Singers, the Rosenbergs and the Shermans, and of course, his very special Nonna Elizabeth, he wanted to be excellent.

So much time and planning had been done by his mother to make sure that everything was perfect. He didn't want to let her down in any way – especially given the events of the last month.

He wanted to do a good job on his *Haftorah* – that portion of the Torah that he was required to learn and then deliver with song in front of a room filled with strangers. He and his friends often referred to it as a barbaric tradition that was endured as a means to an end. The end of course was a large amount of cash – gifts from all those people in attendance. So it was worth the car pools to Hebrew school and Sunday school for three years before the event.

Though his parents were smiling and looking so happy as they hugged their family and friends coming into the Sanctuary, Sam still got a cold stab in his stomach when he remembered how his Dad had looked on that 3rd hole.

Sam had been so terrified that he would lose him. And then the fear had turned to shock when he saw his mother calmly pull a gun out of her purse and shoot Mr. Ramsay. Sam had smiled as he whispered, more to himself that anyone else, "Right on Ma, good job."

Sam still had his dad who was now back in first-class condition – forty-eight hours spent getting "rinsed out" in the hospital saved his life – so nothing else really mattered. Sam never heard his father's jibes at his mother. Grant's voice was clear even in his weakened condition.

"Your mother's boyfriend? That's what you called me? You told him to go ahead and stick the needle in? Your mother's boyfriend?"

Sam also didn't see how his mother had laughed as she leaned over the hospital bed and then climbed in to lie next to his Dad and move her lips all over his face.

Their family doctor suggested to Lisa that Sam should see a psychologist in order to get over his trauma, but Sam took a pass. He was a part of it, he understood what it was about, he knew what was expected of him, he knew the risks, and for sure he knew the rewards if everything worked out. And everything did work out. And he was okay.

Sitting next to Grant and Lisa was Kevin with a big smile on his face, waving at the guests he knew, and even those he didn't know. Despite the difference in their ages, Sam had a deep love and commitment to his brother.

Sitting next to Kevin were Uncle Larry and Nonna Elizabeth. They were holding hands. *Yuck*, thought Sam, *they are sooo old. I wonder if they really do it.*

Behind them sat his new Nonna Lyla – a woman who even at his young age Sam recognized as dynamite, and who he just really liked.

Next to her was Uncle Larry's daughter Meghan, also one of Sam's "chosen" cousins. Meghan had been giving Sam French lessons via the internet these past two years, and while he certainly wasn't fluent, he could speak and understand it enough to get by. Lyla and Meghan hadn't stopped talking to each other since the moment they had sat down.

In the second row were Uncle Johnny and Aunt Marsha and the girls who were still too young to appreciate their cousin Sam's brilliance, or so he thought. Sam knew what Johnny and Peter's business was all about, but after the last month, the bonds between all of them went beyond words. Their love and loyalty to him and to each other was a commitment that would stay with Sam all of his life.

Next to them were Uncle Peter and Aunt Angela and their girls who were still young enough to want to stand up and "see what is going on" rather than just sit quietly. He had seen those two in action in Church when he had gone with Nonna Elizabeth last Christmas and he smiled.

Right up there with them was Uncle Matthew, wearing his "black bibby" as Sam used to call it when he was very little. He had heard him teasing Mom about how he might be forced to kneel down in the *Shul* and cross himself.

You can do anything you want Uncle Matt, thought Sam. *And I know that whatever you do, it will always be right.*

Sam would never know about the directive that Elizabeth had given to her two sons just before he was born. Peter and Matthew had been playing pool when she walked in and insisted that they stop because she had something important to tell them.

"I'm going to say this once and only once," she said. "And after that, we will not raise the subject again.

"Lisa Sherman is pregnant. The father is Grant Teasdale, and he doesn't know about this baby nor does Lisa want to tell him. She is moving into our house next week and will probably be here for a long time. That child will be my grandchild and a part of this family – not by blood, but by love and commitment. I expect the two of you to treat Lisa with respect and that once the baby is here, you will always treat *him or her as one of our own. Hopefully, love between all of you will follow. If not for Lisa's mother Rebecca, none of us would be alive today. Never forget that!"*

Sitting in the third row was David Awasake, one of the heroes during this past month. David had invited Sam to join him on a journey back to his Métis roots. They were going to go to Western Canada and follow the old path of David's ancestors. It was his bar mitzvah gift and Sam was so excited that his parents had given their permission for him to go.

Jennifer White was sitting next to David. Sam knew how important she had also been in saving his parents. Without her, today would not be the celebration that it was going to be.

Sitting near the back of the Sanctuary were Sam's friends from Boston Latin – fifteen guys and ten girls to be exact, along with Mr. Hazelton, his home room teacher, and Mr. Hazelton's partner. Sam had insisted that he bring him along and both men were very appreciative at being included in this celebration.

The service was just about to begin. Sam and his parents walked up to the Ark and the Rabbi removed the Torah. He handed it to Sam who then turned to face the congregation.

"*Shma Yisroel, Adonai elohayno, adonai ached.*"

Two hours later everyone was in the social hall getting ready to have lunch. Grant and Lisa were chatting with guests when Sam came over accompanied by three of his friends.

"Mom, Dad, I would like you to meet these friends who enrolled in school only six months ago," he said. "Jack Gold, Ryan Kelly and Rhonda Cohen."

"Oh Rhonda," said Grant as his face lit up. "Sam has told me so many great things about you. It's nice to finally meet you in person." Lisa noticed the look of horror on Sam's face and willed herself to keep a straight face.

"Grant, you idiot!" she whispered when the kids had moved away. "Sam nearly passed out right in front of us. He didn't want Rhonda to know that he's been talking about her to you – his father."

"Uh oh," said Grant with a sheepish grin on his face. "I didn't think of that. Should I say something to Sam?"

"No, you've said enough," she answered, patting him on the shoulder. "Don't you remember what it was like to be a teenager and to want to be cool and macho?"

As soon as the words were out of her mouth Lisa grabbed Grant's hand and apologized. "I'm sorry, darling, I forgot."

Grant smiled and said, "I'm glad you forgot. For a minute, so did I. Thanks to you, my life today is all that there is."

Lisa walked out of the ladies room and into the arms of Johnny Brattini. They hugged and walked over to the champagne bar to have a drink and chat.

"Today is not the day for hokey confessions, *mea culpas* or any words of unrequited love," said Johnny. "But in a few weeks, when things are settled down, we need to speak. I know you're involved with Grant, but I am not going to go quietly into the night."

"Holy cow," laughed Lisa. "When did you decide to take up novel writing?"

"Very funny, Lisa," answered Johnny. "Here I am, trying to have a mature and non-confrontational conversation with you and you're mixing me up."

"You're right. That's not fair," said Lisa, "especially since you and your funny bunny men saved my son. Now I'll have to be nice to you forever. How then can we continue to have the fights we used to and gamble on the football games that we used to, which I usually won, by the way?"

Johnny just looked at her. He couldn't think of the right words to tell her how he felt. When Lisa had calmly pulled a gun out of her purse on that fairway and had blown Ramsay's head off, it was almost déjà vu – she had the same look in her eyes that her late mother Rebecca had so many years ago when she had aimed a gun at his own head and fired it.

Lisa looked into his eyes and saw what was there. She decided it was time to do the talking for both of them…and to do it right now.

"Johnny, this is the kind of conversation best spoken in a quiet lounge with a glass of wine," she said. "But I can see from your face that this is going to have to be the right moment."

Johnny nodded his head but said nothing.

"You and I knew right from the outset that there was never going to be anywhere for us to go together," she said quietly as she took his hand.

"Don't think I didn't notice how cute you were when I saw you waiting for me at the airport, so many years ago." Johnny liked hearing that and his face showed it.

"But we both knew that there was no way for us to make it work, ever, and nothing is ever going to happen to change that reality."

Johnny stayed silent. Lisa wished that he would say something, even if it wasn't what she wanted to hear. But the look in his eyes prompted her to continue.

"Johnny, as long as we both acknowledge it, we can continue to be the loving friends and occasional verbal sparring partners that we've both enjoyed being to each other these past years. But the reality of Grant in my life is not negotiable. He is the father of my son and I love him.

"You know that I also have a love for all of you that can never be properly spoken. And as for you and me, I hope that you'll stay my friend and Sam's as well. I don't want to lose you."

Johnny knew that she was right and that there was nothing more to be said, especially by him. She had said it all. She was a very special woman.

"I love you Lisa, in so many ways," he finally whispered as he took her hand. "But in my gut I know that you are absolutely right. Thank you for making it so easy for me to share my feelings with you. Maybe there will be something more for us in the next life. But for now, I accept the reality. So be it."

At seven o'clock, when the family and very close friends had descended on the Tranby house for a dinner party, Grant and Lisa tapped their wine glasses to get everyone's attention before they sat down for dinner.

"Lisa has honoured me by accepting my marriage proposal," said Grant as he put his arm around her. Before the applause could get louder, he continued. "We have checked with Sam and he says that it's okay for us to get married...right now. We hope you don't mind. His wild party with his friends takes place tomorrow so as long as we don't do anything to spoil that, he's happy.

"So without any further delays, this is our moment. Matthew, and Rabbi Dolgin, we thank you both for being here to share in our *Simcha* and also agreeing to jointly officiate at our marriage ceremony. We are so ready."

CHAPTER THIRTY-ONE

It was ladies day at the Toronto Valley Golf Course and the regular morning group of Elly, Barbie, Bertye, Joyce and Linda were making their way towards the infamous 3rd hole – newly designed and still one of the most difficult holes in Ontario as rated by the golf magazine.

Today there were five of them because Elly had broken her ankle and the club had bent their rules and allowed her to ride along on the course with her friends.

"Okay ladies," said Bertye. "Today we are going to take some extra time to avoid hitting into the water. I am going to aim for the middle – doesn't matter how short the drive – I am tired of giving up my golf balls to people with retrievers."

Six strokes each later, including penalty shots, the ladies were at the edge of the green. They tried to chip on to the right side, which would then roll down into some grass, as opposed to the left side, which would then roll into the water.

"Gee, do you remember that brouhaha that went down right here last month?" asked Joyce. "Today, it doesn't look like anything ever happened. I can't even see any junk from that helicopter accident."

"Well, City maintenance crews moved in quickly," said Barbie. "I was here with Steve three days after it happened and there was nothing, absolutely nothing, out of place."

THE THIRD HOLE

She chipped her ball. Unfortunately it was too strong a shot, and though the ball rolled straight up towards the hole, it continued past it over the south edge of the green and then disappeared.

"Forget it Barbie," said Linda. "It's gone."

"Nope, I will not forget it," said Barbie. "I have left too many balls on this hole."

Elly drove the cart around to the right side as Barbie trotted up to the flag and walked past it towards the edge of the green. Joyce, Linda and Bertye were trudging along behind her.

Once at the top of the hill, Barbie turned to her right and started walking slowly down towards the water, keeping her eyes on the ground to make sure she that she didn't trip over any debris or animal dung. Her eye caught the white of a ball a few more yards down the slope.

"I see it!" she yelled as she continued down the hill.

When she lifted her head she saw something else. It was in the water, just to the side and not visible unless someone was standing exactly where she now stood.

"Girls!" she shrieked. "Call 911 – I can't believe it! There's a body in the water! And it has a golf club sticking out of it!"

An hour later, the body of Carl Ashton, Mayor of the city of Toronto was removed from the water surrounding the 3rd hole. Someone had sharpened the shaft of a 9 iron, turning it into a lance, and had then buried it in his stomach. The police guessed that his body had been lying in the water for at least two days. Forensics would tell them for sure, and also tell them if he had been alive when he was thrown in.

Undercover FBI agents Fred Ahmad and Dan Greenberg were sitting in a beige van with the markings of a TV repair company that was parked on the main street just across from St. Constantine Greek Church in Massena, New York. It was close to midnight when a black SUV finally pulled up and stopped in front of the church.

"Our targets have landed," said Ahmad. "Remember Danny boy. No witnesses, no evidence, no nothing. Those are our orders."

"Yah, let's make this a Jennie exercise," said Greenberg with a smile.

The doors to the SUV opened and two men got out carrying a carton that could have held a TV, or anything else that would fit into a 48x48 container. They were each holding one end as they passed in front of the van where Ahmad and Greenberg were now crouched on the floor. The agents opened the back door and quickly jumped out before the Mohawks could react.

Greenberg zapped them, Ahmad slapped duct tape over their mouths and then they threw both of them into the back of the van, along with the container. They knew that it would be full of explosives even before they looked inside to confirm it. It all went down in less than five minutes.

Two other agents soon arrived and "hijacked" the SUV. Twenty minutes later they were all standing inside a depot near the border. Ahmad and Greenberg nodded to the others present before they turned around and left. They wouldn't know and didn't care what would eventually happen to the explosives or the men. Their job was done.

The bodies of Silvana Rackova and Yuri Latchman were discovered under a huge tarpaulin in the back of a storage building just outside of Boston. Both had been alive when they were put into separate containers and liquid cement was poured in up to their necks.

Latchman had lived for another six hours. Silvana lasted for another eight hours.

Life continued on for both the DeLuca and Brattini families – personally and in business. The bond formed between Peter and Johnny was now a reality and there were changes to the operations of both their business interests that recognized it.

Xi Ping Lan was relatively young to be the Chairman of Goldstar Corporation. He was known as "Ping Pong" to his former Harvard classmates, which included Peter DeLuca and his brother Matthew. He had taken over the reins of the company from his father who was now in the first stages of Alzheimer's.

Today, even though he was in the office of Giancarlo Brattini, it was Peter DeLuca who had greeted him at the door with hugs and high-five hand slaps. He had then introduced "my Uncle Johnny" to Ping Pong as Johnny grimaced.

The three men talked for close to two hours before Ping Pong brought the conversation to an end. He knew what the Salerno and Villano families were all about; that's why he was here. He needed their protection, their access to cash and their political connections.

"I'm going back home to Beijing later today," he said. "But if we can work this out, I'll be back as soon as we are ready to talk serious business. Your organizations are our first choice in terms of a joint venture. Keep in mind that our economy has continued to grow in the face of current global meltdowns. Our appetite for natural resources has become more and more voracious – and by natural selection, that leads us to resource-rich Canada.

"The Chinese do not have preconceived ideas about dealing with the aboriginals, and so we are going to go after them, just like a Harvard student in heat."

Peter smiled as he remembered some of their wild times and their even wilder girls.

"We want the First Nations communities," Ping Pong went on "and their resources of oil, gas, mining and lumber developments under our umbrella, and we are prepared to pay for it.

"With open access by the First Nations to cross the borders, we prefer to be located here, in the US. We anticipate no problems moving our interests back and forth."

"Okay buddy," said Peter. "We'll have to meet with our associates, but we'll get back to you very soon.

"And please give your father a hug from Angela and me," he continued. "He showed us such a wonderful time when we were in China two years ago. Fucking Alzheimer's – it's just so unfair."

"It was nice to meet you," said Johnny as he shook hands with Ping Pong. "Your goal and your strategy to reach it is first class. I'm optimistic that we'll be working together soon."

Jennifer White and David Awasake had both been promoted and were now located in Washington, DC. David was the senior RCMP liaison to the FBI – otherwise known as Bob Lantinos. Jennifer was now in the sights of the powers that be to succeed him...eventually. She always knew she had what it would take to become the first female head of the FBI, and now others knew it as well.

She and David were still in the "should we or shouldn't we?" stage of their mutual sexual attraction. Jennie had always tried to avoid these kinds of situations because of the problems they caused. But she was hot – and so was he.

"Here's my plan," she said to him one night when they were out for dinner. "Let's agree to have one night followed by one day of unrestricted sex – do anything, say anything – and then we'll return to being professional associates and we won't ever do it again."

"What a brilliant idea," said David grinning as he motioned for the bill. "Let's go."

Elizabeth DeLuca had decided to move to Toronto to be with Larry Lyons. After so many years of turmoil she was determined to let nothing keep her from being right next to him until the road came to its end.

Elizabeth had also reconciled Lyla's approach to life with her own. The two women, both stunning and chic, both with excellent taste and both sharing a deep love for their special man, knew that they would always work it out – whatever it might be. Larry was completely happy and at peace.

Matthew DeLuca continued his work in the Vatican and was one of the young priests being monitored as a potential leader. He knew a lot more about his family's interests than they hoped he did, but for him, the service he gave to his God and to his Church was all that mattered.

Grant and Lisa Teasdale and their son Sam were saying good bye to Kevin at the Christopher Robin Home. They had just spent a week in Disneyworld as part of their family honeymoon, and it was time for

Kevin to get back to his own life. It had been a very eventful month, and even though he had participated in all the family celebrations, Kevin was ready to settle back into the familiar environment that he had always known and where he was surrounded by the best that his life could give him.

"Bye Mommy Lisa, Daddy and Sam," said Kevin just as he started running up the driveway towards his friends in the playground off to the right of the Home.

"See you!" he waved without turning back.

During their flight back to Boston, the Teasdale family continued their discussions about their new life – primarily where they should settle down.

To leave Boston? Sam would soon be finished at the Boston Latin School so it would be no problem for him to move. He was confident and happy and would always find friends.

To live in Florida?

Lisa could try to move her photography operation down there. Would it work?

To leave Florida?

Could Grant move his private security services up to Boston? Would it be too much of a hassle for his clients? And what about Kevin?

What about somewhere in between?

EPILOGUE

The four old friends sitting around the table having lunch were laughing. They had first met when they were ten years old and were assigned to the same cabin at the Northland Camp in New Hampshire. They had connected positively right away, especially when one of them, Jake Bartoli, was being bullied – something that the other three soon ended. Jake was a little person with achondroplasia dwarfism and immediately became the mascot of his new friends, Bob Lantinos, Billy Walker, and Brian Gilley. They decided to share all of Jake's physical limitations and after five years together at camp, their friendship was solidified for the rest of their lives.

After high school they had tried to get into the same college but it didn't work out. Jake Bartoli and Bob Lantinos made it into Harvard; Billy Walker's parents had moved their family to Halifax, Nova Scotia years earlier, so he attended Dalhousie University, and Brian Gilley, who would eventually become the president of the United States, barely made it into NYU.

When they were together in a relaxed, unofficial circumstance as they were today, they reverted to their youth – good buddies with an intense loyalty to each other and no restrictions on their conversation.

Jake Bartoli had just given them a report of his telephone conversation earlier that morning with Aviva Berens, the prime minister of Israel. She had been complaining that the recent joint FBI–INSETs success story had not involved any of her people even though it had involved her country. All she got for the exercise was one bad guy – The Deputy Minister of Finance, Shlomo Rakowski.

"Hey, how come none of the good guys were one of my people?" she had asked Jake who had already started laughing. "You know I have a standard to maintain. And is it true that Mr. Mossad himself let your undercovers into my tiny country?"

As if you didn't know, *thought Jake.*

"*And for that I didn't even get a token present. In case it slipped your mind, I am the head honcho here my American Prince and don't you ever forget it. You owe me. So, I do love those chocolate cupcakes from that Washington bakery. Feel free to send me some to express your appreciation.*"

"I assume you have already taken care of it, Jake," laughed President Gilly as he got up and walked over to the window furtively taking a cigarette out of his pocket and lighting it. "Of course, Aviva is coming to Washington for a Middle East conference in three weeks."

"Hey, I've never met her!" said Billy. "I hear she's dynamite. So what about an FBI – Mountie lunch meeting? What do you say Bob? I'll bring dessert."

"There seems to be no proper rules of order when we get together," laughed Lantinos. "Okay Billy, since your prime minister will also be here for that meeting, you can assign yourself as his security. I'll make sure to introduce you properly. How does this sound?

"Madame Prime Minister, may I present William Walker, Superintendent of the Royal Canadian Mounted Police. He is a devout Catholic, but I am sure he knows enough about Judaism to make it through the night. Once upon a time he was the worst kid in camp, but now he is the boss of those guys in red jackets that you see on cereal boxes chasing after bears and wolves in the Arctic."

"Bad," laughed Billy. "Besides, my prime minister is a real fan of hers, and I have no doubt that she knows all there is to know about Canada."

President Gilley, who was still standing next to the window, laughing, opened it just a sliver and threw his cigarette butt out.

"Boo," was the combined hiss of the others.

"Okay," said the president, ignoring them. "I have another three years in this office so there is no need for me to be overly nice to any of you. Smarten up! Now, let's talk about the 3rd Hole exercise – off the record."

The successful undercover operation of the FBI – INSETs task force, reinforced by the Italian component, had also given the good guys the probable cause needed to get the evidence from other countries besides the United States and Canada, namely Serbia, Italy, France and quietly, very quietly, Russia. Seized computers, internet traces, telephone tracking – the usual subpoenas properly exercised and useable in court.

Shlomo Rakowski, Israel's Deputy Minister of Finance was one of those exposed as a part of Howard Ramsay's cabal of evil. He had provided Ramsay with false names, immigration files and false affidavits in order to secretly transfer laundered money and illegal immigrants into Israel and then into Canada and the United States. He also provided Ramsay with information about who was under investigation for money laundering in Israel and what evidence they had. He had also created the diamond haven that Latchman used in his smuggling operations and which Rakowski had a twenty-five percent piece of.

When Rakowski's body had been found with a plastic bag tied around his head, suicide was how the Israeli government chose to handle it. And that file was now closed.

Aviva Berens had begun her career as a Mossad agent, recruited because of her Russian background and her gift of the gab when it came to the Russian Refuseniks – specifically those planted by the KGB to act as informants. When she came to the end of the line in terms of how far a woman could move up the ladder of Mossad's leadership, she decided to switch to politics, and the rest is history. Golda Meir had been a fearless leader of Israel forty years earlier and it had taken this long for another woman to step up to the plate.

But Prime Minister Berens was more than a successful politician. She was, and probably still could be, a skilled operative who had killed several enemies of Israel during her career. She did not fit the usual mould of female politicians, even those who were at the top of the heap. She was single by choice, irreverent, decisive and absolutely charming – when she wanted to be charming. She was only five foot three, had brown eyes and brown hair. She often joked about her being twenty pounds overweight even though it was probably closer to thirty pounds. Getting detailed information on her background was impossible, or at least impossible for anyone other than the president of the United States.

"Aviva Berens' mother, Olga Berenofsky, was married to the Soviet Minister of Justice," said President Gilley as he started munching on some grapes. "At the same time she was also the lover of Boris Latchman, and the conduit through which he moved his diamond operation."

"Holy shit!" gasped Lantinos. "Talk about a major puzzle piece falling into place."

"There's more," said Gilley as he started on some tangerines. "Latchman tried to get Olga out of Russia once he realized that their cover was broken. Her daughter Aviva had already emigrated to Israel years earlier and was a Likud member of the Knesset. Latchman knew that Yeltsin would be in a rage when he found out about the affair and he became desperate. He had maintained contact with a young KGB agent – Russia's current president – who almost managed to get Olga out – he was with her at the Minsk train station when Yeltsin's guys caught up to them. They shot her in the face before they took off. She was dead before she hit the ground. It took ten years, but all the assassins have now met their maker."

"Well, that explains the new and special friendship between the president and the prime minister," said Jake, "as well as the camaraderie between Russia and Israel. Very interesting."

No one spoke for a few minutes.

"Well Mr. President," Billy Walker finally said with a big smile on his face, "let's lighten up the mood here. Now that we know where the best source of information is located, how about letting me set up a direct line for the Mounties?"

"Get in line Billy," laughed Bob Lantinos, "me first. Especially since both Jennifer White and Larry Lyons are mine."

"Yes, but Awasake is mine!" said Walker. "And I hear rumours about him and Jennifer. Wow, what a hoot that would be!"

"No incest in our top agencies," chortled the president, "let's hope they fuck themselves into remission." He then poured everyone some more wine.

"Now Bob, didn't you tell me that you wanted to retire?" he asked. "Though I can't imagine what you would do to amuse yourself."

"Bob thinks he's missed his calling," laughed Bartoli. "He wants to become a mystery writer. This last exercise between the Italians, the aboriginals, the Sicilians and now maybe even the Chinese, is totally taking over his life."

"Very funny, you jerk," said Lantinos, trying not to smile. "But nailing all those senior bureaucrats, along with Berens' favourite Deputy Minister of Finance, plus – wait for it – our own former FBI director, could never have happened without our giving the carte blanche that we did to those young whippersnappers. And modesty prevents me from reminding you all whose idea it was to do just that."

"Whippersnappers? What is that word?" howled Gilley. "Are we still in the Truman era? What's with you Bob – are you losing it?"

Before he could answer, Gilley continued in a more serious tone. "No retirement for you yet, Bob. I need you to step up for the next two years. I want to make sure that your successor won't slip off the edge like Jackson. I even have someone in mind."

"If you're thinking of Larry Lyons, forget it," said Lantinos. "He and Elizabeth DeLuca are together in the true sense of the word. Nothing will change the fact that she is the widow of one of the major crime bosses of the last fifty years, and that will always be part of his résumé."

"I wasn't thinking of him," smiled the president. "I was thinking of her."

"Woof, woof!" laughed Bartoli. "Oh, she is so not like a G-man. And my head, specifically my mouth, comes up to guess what part of her fabulous body? Thank the Lord for my iron resistance."

Bob Lantinos was quiet. Is it possible? A female FBI chief? Only if none of Jennifer's past exploits come back to haunt her – definitely not a certainty, that's for sure.

"Well, you know what I think about her Brian," said Bob after a few minutes. "And if you are serious, I'll stay on – and also take a personal hand in her orientation. But I'm not sure sitting behind a desk will work for her."

"I wasn't kidding about Awasake," jibed Billy Walker. "Right now they're playing the cheetah game with each other. But if it gets more serious, then you'll have to step in, Bob. Can you handle the drama? I mean, they are like two animals in heat."

"Well, it's too early to worry about that," said Gilley. "Let's just follow the normal process. Okay with you Bob?"

"Okay with me," he answered.

"Now, I just want to tell you again what a great job you all did on this latest project," said President Gilley. "Too bad the public will never know how close we all came to a disaster. Well done!

"Now, let's have some cognac and more dessert, and after that we can play gin rummy – ten cents a point."

Iguana Books
iguanabooks.com

If you enjoyed *The Third Hole*...
Look for other books coming soon from Iguana Books! Subscribe to our blog for updates as they happen.

iguanabooks.com/blog/

You can also learn more about Patti Starr and her upcoming work on her blog.

patriciastarr.com

If you're a writer ...
Iguana Books is always looking for great new writers, in every genre. We produce primarily ebooks but, as you can see, we do the occasional print book as well. Visit us at iguanabooks.com to see what Iguana Books has to offer both emerging and established authors.

iguanabooks.com/publishing-with-iguana/

If you're looking for another good book ...
All Iguana Books books are available on our website. We pride ourselves on making sure that every Iguana book is a great read.

iguanabooks.com/bookstore/

Visit our bookstore today and support your favourite author.

CPSIA information can be obtained at www.ICGtesting.com
Printed in the USA
LVOW100539110413

328583LV00007B/24/P

9 781927 403594